"TURN AND FACE ME,
YOU WOMAN-KILLER!"

Pickney turned and said in a tight voice, "This is just me and him, everybody. Just me and the Gunsmith."

Clint did not wait for Pickney to start the play. Instead, his hand flashed down and the Colt in his holster jumped as if it were a live thing. Pickney was lightning fast, too.

Pickney's gun had cleared leather, but it was still pointing down when the man pulled the trigger. Clint unleashed three slugs and each one rocked Pickney back until his arms extended wide and he crashed backward through the glass window he had already busted.

Don't miss any of the lusty, hard-riding action
in the Jove Western series,
THE GUNSMITH

MACKLIN'S WOMEN
THE CHINESE GUNMEN
THE WOMAN HUNT
THE GUNS OF ABILENE
THREE GUNS FOR GLORY
LEADTOWN
THE LONGHORN WAR
QUANAH'S REVENGE
HEAVYWEIGHT GUN
NEW ORLEANS FIRE
ONE-HANDED GUN
THE CANADIAN PAYROLL
DRAW TO AN INSIDE DEATH
DEAD MAN'S HAND
BANDIT GOLD
BUCKSKINS AND SIX-GUNS
SILVER WAR
HIGH NOON AT LANCASTER
BANDIDO BLOOD
THE DODGE CITY GANG
SASQUATCH HUNT
BULLETS AND BALLOTS
THE RIVERBOAT GANG
KILLER GRIZZLY
NORTH OF THE BORDER
EAGLE'S GAP
CHINATOWN HELL
THE PANHANDLE SEARCH
WILDCAT ROUNDUP
THE PONDEROSA WAR
TROUBLE RIDES A FAST HORSE
DYNAMITE JUSTICE
THE POSSE
NIGHT OF THE GILA
THE BOUNTY WOMEN
BLACK PEARL SALOON
GUNDOWN IN PARADISE
KING OF THE BORDER

THE EL PASO SALT WAR
THE TEN PINES KILLER
HELL WITH A PISTOL
THE WYOMING CATTLE KILL
THE GOLDEN HORSEMAN
THE SCARLET GUN
NAVAHO BILL
WILD BILL'S GHOST
THE MINER'S SHOWDOWN
ARCHER'S REVENGE
SHOWDOWN IN RATON
WHEN LEGENDS MEET
DESERT HELL
THE DIAMOND GUN
DENVER DUO
HELL ON WHEELS
THE LEGEND MAKER
WALKING DEAD MAN
CROSSFIRE MOUNTAIN
THE DEADLY HEALER
THE TRAIL DRIVE WAR
GERONIMO'S TRAIL
THE COMSTOCK GOLD FRAUD
BOOM TOWN KILLER
TEXAS TRACKDOWN
THE FAST DRAW LEAGUE
SHOWDOWN IN RIO MALO
OUTLAW TRAIL
HOMESTEADER GUNS
FIVE CARD DEATH
TRAILDRIVE TO MONTANA
TRIAL BY FIRE
THE OLD WHISTLER GANG
DAUGHTER OF GOLD
APACHE GOLD
PLAINS MURDER
DEADLY MEMORIES

And coming next month:

THE GUNSMITH #77: NEW MEXICO SHOWDOWN

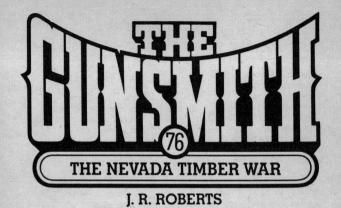

THE GUNSMITH

76

THE NEVADA TIMBER WAR

J. R. ROBERTS

JOVE BOOKS, NEW YORK

THE GUNSMITH #76: THE NEVADA TIMBER WAR

A Jove book / published by arrangement with
the author

PRINTING HISTORY
Jove edition/ April 1988

ISBN: 0-515-09523-0

Jove books are published by The Berkley Publishing Group,
200 Madison Avenue, New York, New York 10016.
The name ''JOVE'' and the ''J'' logo
are trademarks belonging to Jove Publications, Inc.

PRINTED IN THE UNITED STATES OF AMERICA

10 9 8 7 6 5 4 3 2 1

ONE

By midnight there was a huge crowd of spectators bunched around the poker table, where Clint had already dropped two thousand dollars. And although it was not at all unusual for John Casey to fleece his clients, no one in Fallon, Nevada, had expected that the big saloon owner would ever dare to cheat the Gunsmith. That sort of thing could get you killed right sudden, and even though Casey was a mighty good man with a gun or knife, most of the crowd watching figured he was flirting with death.

Clint Adams was more curious than angry. For seven hours, he had been playing cards, and during most of that time, he had been winning. Clint was a first-rate gambler and made no pretense about it. He figured if someone asked him about his skill at poker, faro, or monte, and he told them that he could match most professionals, then his conscience was clear and he had nothing to hide or worry about. It was no fun to beat some sodbuster or half-drunk cowboy who had sweated and worked from sunup to sundown for thirty dollars a month. Clint would decline to take their money—unless they insisted. And there were many men who figured it was worth dropping a month's wages just to be able to brag that they had sat down at the same poker table with the famed Gunsmith. That was fine. But cheating was another matter. Clint figured he was a professional and so was John Casey. And if the game had been on the square, he would have walked away from it hours ago with the full knowledge that his luck was running bad and that he would have another chance at the huge, red-bearded saloon owner.

1

"How many cards you need?" Casey grunted.

Clint looked at his hand and slapped down a pair. "Two."

The cards seemed to jump out of Casey's fist as if they were alive. The man smiled and said, "Maybe your luck is due for a change. I guess these folks should have warned you that I'm a pretty fair poker player."

"Oh," Clint drawled, "I could see that all by myself after the first hand. I was more interested in how many derringers you're packing."

Casey's smile froze on his broad, meaty face. He was a heavyset man in his early forties who considered himself a dandy, with his starched white collar and black suit and big gold rings on both of his hands. His red mustache was long and waxed at the tips and two beautiful dancehall girls stood just slightly behind him with their hands on each of his wide shoulders.

"One derringer," Casey said, "is plenty enough firepower to do the job."

"I would think so," Clint said with an easy smile as he tossed another fifty dollars into the pot and saw that he had three fives. "But you're packing two derringers and a belly gun."

The skin around Casey's eyes tightened and he studied his hand. "I understand you're a pretty fair man with a gun yourself. I'll take your fifty dollars and raise you another hundred."

Clint studied his dwindling pile of chips. He was down to less than two hundred dollars. He'd started the game early in the afternoon with that much but had built his winnings up to better than two thousand. And then John Casey had invited himself into the game. Clint had been losing steadily ever since.

"Call you," Clint said, pitching in his chips. "I've got three fives."

Casey almost looked sad. "Damn shame I have to tell you this, Gunsmith, but I've got three tens." After showing his cards, Casey's big hands reached forward and he scooped up the pot and pulled it across the green felt table to his place beside him. The two girls moved over and began to make a big show of giggling and showing their cleavage. They would stack the chips into neat little piles while the other customers ogled them and grinned. Pure show business and equally pure bullshit.

Casey shook his head. As soon as the chips were stacked, he pushed a generous pile of them at the Gunsmith and said, "There's five hundred dollars, Mr. Adams. Why don't you take them, and we'll have ourselves a drink to show that there is no hard feelings and that my saloon is generous. It just hasn't been your night. We'll have a drink and—"

Clint's voice hardened. "I've still got some chips and I'll play them off. I think maybe I've figured out your little game, Casey. And if you're doing what I think you're doing, you're going to need that five hundred dollars to pay off your doctor's bills when I finish with you."

Casey did not like that. His normal complexion was red but his face turned almost purple with rage. Clint saw his eyes dart across the room in a signal, and the Gunsmith knew that Casey's men were getting into position to use their weapons if there was trouble. The crowd knew it as well and the savvy ones stepped back until they formed a wide circle around the table.

"Your men will probably get me from behind," Clint said evenly, "but not until I've put a bullet through your brisket."

Casey began to sweat profusely. The saloon was hot and the air was thick with cigar smoke. There had not been a breath of fresh air inside since the last man had walked outside and that had been some time ago. Clint smiled, "You're sweating. Don't get the cards wet."

The Gunsmith reached for his own handkerchief. It was dirty and rumpled; no gentleman would have touched it unless he was drunk. "You can use this."

John Casey was forced to reach for his own handkerchief tucked neatly in his front coat pocket. It was silk and mono-grammed with his initials, but Clint paid little attention to anything other than the fact that Casey reached for it with his left hand—and Casey was right-handed. The Gunsmith knew that he finally had his answer. Casey didn't mark cards and he didn't have a spotter standing behind, signaling Clint's hand. Casey was using some kind of holdout. A holdout was a mechanical device of some kind that usually included wires and pulleys. It was strapped to a man's forearm and extended a card into its wearer's palm whenever he bent his elbow. Then, when the arm was straightened, it retreated back up the gambler's sleeve. In his years of gambling, Clint had seen all sorts of holdout mechanisms, some that worked so smoothly that they were almost impossible for even a professional like himself to detect, but others so clumsy that they had the fatal flaw of pitching cards out when least expected. That could get the wearer of a holdout killed because the mechanism itself was indisputable evidence of cheating. A man might deal from the bottom of the deck or have a few hidden cards and then talk his way out of trouble, but he was trapped with a holdout up his sleeve.

"Deal," Casey said. "This hand is for all you've got left. Agreed?"

"Agreed," Clint said. He shuffled the deck then pushed it across the table. "Cut."

The saloon owner cut the cards, and Clint took them back and dealt out five. He didn't even look at his own cards, but kept his eyes on the hulking figure across from him. "How many?"

"One," Casey snapped, mopping his face again with his left hand. The girls had moved away from their boss. The crowd seemed to hold its breath under the cloud of blue smoke. "Ain't you even going to look at your own goddam cards?" Casey shouted. "What are you staring at me for?"

"My cards don't matter anymore," Clint said in an easy voice. "What matters right now is whether you want to lose your life or your money. That's the choice I'm offering."

The spectators scattered. Some headed for the front door, others ducked behind tables or packed in behind the bar.

Casey laid his hands flat on the tabletop. "I've got men behind you, and I know that you don't want to die any more than I do. So why don't you take the money I just offered and get the hell out of my place while you still can."

But Clint shook his head. "It can't be that easy," he said. "You're using a holdout and I want everyone in this place to see it. I'm sure it's something real clever. It isn't strapped to your arm. Nope, I think it's one of those kind that are strapped to your legs."

"You're crazy!" Casey started to reach to signal his men, but Clint's hand shot down and his gun came up as he yelled, "Anybody back there goes for his gun, I'll kill your boss!"

"Don't move!" Casey whispered as the two saloon girls shot out the front door in a rush with most of the crowd.

Clint eased out of his chair. He put his back to the wall, and now he could see three gunmen standing by ready to draw. Clint said, "You fellas got two choices: walk, or draw and die. Which is it going to be?"

The gunmen didn't have much trouble reaching a decision. They knew that Clint Adams was one of the deadliest men that had ever pulled a Colt out of a holster. "We'll walk," the tallest of the three said. "But what about Mr. Casey?"

"Since you're not employed by him, that isn't your concern any longer, is it?"

The three nodded and left. Clint glanced at the bartender and a few of those that had not left the saloon—either because they were too scared to move or too dumb to know better. "Everybody just stay still and don't get to moving around." Clint turned to the saloon owner and his voice was as hard as obsidian. "Casey, stand up."

Casey stood. He kept his hands on the table so there was no mistaking his intention not to draw.

Clint grinned. "Now, unbuckle your belt and unbutton your pants. Let 'em drop to your ankles."

"Goddam you!" the man hissed. "I'll get you for this."

"You don't understand," Clint said. "A lot of that pile of chips resting on your side of the table belongs to me. Now do as I say."

John Casey had no choice. He unbuckled his belt and the

belly gun clattered to the floor. It was a Colt .44 with the barrel cut off almost flush with the cylinder. A belly gun was inaccurate even across a room. But it could be concealed behind a man's belt and it sure as hell was accurate across a poker table.

"Let 'em drop!" Clint growled.

Casey dropped his pants. Clint and everyone else in the room stared at the contraption the big saloon owner wore. There were two small metal plates about the size of money clips strapped to the insides of his thighs. They were attached by wires that ran up and under his shirt and coat.

"Damn fancy," Clint said, with admiration. "Let's see the rest of it."

"You've seen enough!" Casey roared. "If you've a mind to shoot me, then do it! Otherwise, go to hell!"

"All right," Clint said. Without appearing to aim, he moved his gun a fraction, and it roared as a bullet passed through the back of Casey's right hand and buried itself into the green felt tabletop.

"Ahhh!" the saloon owner screamed, grabbing his shattered hand. He staggered backward, tripping over the pants gathered around his ankles, and crashed onto the sawdust floor.

Clint said, "Hold up your other hand. I want to see if I can shoot off a finger. Gonna make damn sure that you never use another holdout or double-deal another hand of cards."

The man's composure broke down completely. "Goddammit, you win!" he cried, pushing himself clumsily to his feet and ripping off his jacket, then his shirt.

When the man was undressed except for his underpants, the Gunsmith shook his head and said, "Why, that's the fanciest damn holdout I ever saw in my life. What's it called?"

"Kepplinger Holdout," Casey shouted in anger and pain.

"Where'd you get it?"

"San Francisco's Barbary Coast." Casey shook his head. "Damn thing cost me almost three thousand dollars."

Clint stepped forward. The Kepplinger Holdout was an

ingenious connection of wires and pulleys that ended up with a card feeder strapped to the man's forearm. Most professionals looked for the bending or unbending of the elbow to feed a holdout, but not with the Kepplinger, and that was what had thrown the Gunsmith all evening. With the Kepplinger, all Casey had needed to do in order to get a hidden card was spread his legs a fraction of an inch.

The mechanism itself was beautifully crafted and some of the mechanical parts were constructed out of gold plating and teakwood. "It's a work of art," Clint said with real admiration. "Take if off."

Hope flared in Casey's eyes. "You want it, it's yours! It never fails."

"It failed tonight," Clint said. He waited until Casey unstrapped the entire works from his powerful body before he said, "Throw it over here on the floor. Nice and easy."

Casey did as he was told. Clint bent down and picked the Kepplinger Holdout up and then he holstered his six-gun. Casey was too naked to have anything hidden and too fat to move quick enough to reach his pants with his only good hand.

"Three thousand dollars, you say?"

"That's right. Take it and go!"

Clint stared at the device, and his lips curled into a line of contempt. He gripped the holdout, and then he tore it apart, yanked the cables and wires from the plates and the teakwood parts, and threw the entire mess down on the floor.

"Hey!" Casey screeched. "That's three thousand dollars!"

"Was three thousand," the Gunsmith said as he used his heel to grind the remains into the sawdust.

Casey looked as if he were about to weep. Clint had no pity for the man. He yelled for the bartender to come and get the poker chips and bring him back cash. "Try anything funny," he warned, "and I'll grab one of those wires and use it on you like a necktie."

"Yes, sir!" the bartender said, hurriedly scooping up the chips. A moment later he was back with a bundle of cash. "You can count it, Mr. Gunsmith."

"Won't be necessary," Clint said as pleasant as could be. He turned back and addressed the saloon owner. "Casey, I'm going to trust that you've seen the light and are going to change your evil ways. Everyone left in this room saw the holdout. I'd say your business is about to take a drastic falling off once the word gets out about how you cheat your customers."

Casey glowered at Clint. "You ever come through Fallon again and I'll see that you are buried here!"

"Well, you do have a nice cemetery," Clint said. "But there are a few others I've seen that I like better. Besides, I don't figure on checking out of this world for a good while yet. I'm on my way to San Francisco for some fun. And if some other foolish fella like yourself tries to use one of those Kepplinger things, why, I'll treat him about the same way as I did you."

Clint stuffed the money into his coat and headed for the door. He was almost there when someone yelled, "Look out!"

Clint spun and fired in one smooth action. John Casey had the belly gun up but his only shot was wide to his left. Clint's bullet caught the saloon owner square in the chest and knocked him over backward. He was dead before he hit the floor.

Clint holstered his gun. He looked at the white-faced spectators and said, "You all saw that I killed that card cheat in self-defense. Now, I'd say that Mr. Casey had some Irish in him and would like nothing better than for you boys to have a little wake in honor of his untimely passing. Drinks on the house, bartender!"

"Yes, sir!"

Clint left the saloon and headed for his horse. People out on the boardwalk stared until they realized that the drinks inside were free. Then they stampeded into the saloon like a herd of crazed longhorn cattle, while the Gunsmith stuffed his saddlebags with greenbacks, mounted his horse, Duke, and rode out of Fallon toward the towering Sierra Nevada Mountains and the blue Pacific Ocean far beyond.

TWO

Clint Adams was six miles east of Pine Bluff, Nevada when Duke threw a shoe and went lame. The Gunsmith dismounted at once and saw that his big black gelding had also sustained a rock bruise. He knew that it might take a couple of weeks before the gelding was fit to climb the rocky slopes that would take them around Lake Tahoe.

"Well, Duke," he said, "I guess we're going to just have to take the last few miles a little slower than I'd expected. But we almost reached the mountains."

They had, for a fact. Coming out of the barren, high desert country, they had arrived at the eastern edge of lush Nevada valleys fed by the Truckee and Carson rivers and a number of small Sierra streams. This was good country: Fine stands of timber braced the eastern slopes for hundreds of miles, and Clint could see distant cattle ranches dotting the valleys between Mormon Station and Pine Bluff. Clint had not been through Pine Bluff for several years. But back then there had been a saloon called the Double Eagle, where a pretty girl named Dora worked. Dora had been a fine young filly, and they had enjoyed each other's company. But hell, Clint thought, Dora is probably married by now with a couple of kids and a jealous husband.

Clint loosened Duke's cinch, left his tied reins over the gelding's powerful neck, and man and horse started walking. He could see a lumber mill down on the Carson River, but it was farther south than he intended to walk, so he just set his sights for Pine Bluff and wondered if he was going to make it before sundown.

Two hours later, he knew that he would not. That was the way with distances. What he had figured was six miles had turned out to be nearer fifteen, and as the sun dove into the Sierra peaks, he still had five to go. Clint shared every horseman's aversion to walking. His high-heeled riding boots were not made for anything but to fit through a pair of stirrups. There were a lot of cowboys who would figure that it would not hurt to ride a rock-bruised horse a few miles, but Clint wasn't taking any chances. If it came to that, he'd have walked a hundred miles through Death Valley before causing Duke any unnecessary discomfort. This horse was special, and he'd lost track of all the times Duke had pulled his bacon out of the fire. Why, Duke had outrun Indians, outlaws and — more times than Clint cared to admit — a jealous husband.

Sunset came quickly in western Nevada, and the colors were spectacular as the dying rays of sunshine gilded the peaks so that they looked as if they were lined with beaten copper and gold. Clint stopped and so admired the spectacular colors that he didn't even see the wagon road and the team that halted to let him catch up and hitch a ride.

"Hey, there!" the driver yelled. "You want to stand there all night or would you like a ride into Pine Bluff?"

Clint spun around, embarrassed and chagrined to discover he'd been too absorbed in the beauty of nature not to hear a wagon and team of horses. He was an ex-sheriff and a man with a reputation for his speed and skill with a six-gun. There were just too damn many enemies and wet-behind-the-ears young reputation-seekers to let his guard down, even out in the wide-open spaces. But this man looked like a farmer. He wore bib overalls and a floppy hat. His feet were encased in round-toed work boots, and his hands were large and so thick-fingered that he could not have drawn a gun and fired in a hurry if his life depended upon it. He was in his mid- or late twenties, strong-looking with a lantern jaw and wide cheekbones. His face was deeply tanned as were the backs of his hands, and he was angular and as lean as leather.

Clint wiggled his toes and felt a pain in his feet from the unaccustomed walking. "I sure would appreciate a lift into town," he said. "I'm about to peter out and make a camp right where I stand. But it's hard being so close to town and knowing there's good food and a soft featherbed at the hotel."

The farmer grinned. "I wouldn't know about no soft featherbed. And as for the food, it's just passable and damned expensive. Tie your horse to the back and hop on up."

Clint was more than happy to oblige. "My name is Clint Adams," he said, introducing himself.

"Abner Turner. You can probably figure out by the smell of me that I raise sheep hereabouts. Run a flock of about five thousand and try to do a little farming. But mostly, I'm a sheepman."

"That's a lot of woolies," Clint said, taking the man's rough hand and indeed smelling the strong scent of sheep and greasy wool. "This is also pretty good cattle and logging country, too, isn't it?"

Turner nodded. "That's the problem, almost everyone wants a piece of it and there are too many that want it all."

"I saw a big timber mill operating a few miles south of here on the Carson River."

At the mention of timber the driver's face stiffened. "I can deal with the cattlemen just fine," he said. "They look upon a sheepman as scum but they respect my property rights and know that I can stop their irrigation water before it leaves my land. If it weren't for the fact that my Pa was one of the first to settle in this valley and I inherited his water rights, I'd be in deep trouble. But as it is, I have some power and I treat the cattlemen fair enough."

"But I can tell from the tone of your voice that the loggers are a different story."

Turner nodded emphatically. "Damn right they are! They're trying to run me out of this valley, and I'll be damned if I'll let them. The only thing that worries me is my Milly."

"Milly?"

"Yeah," he said, face softening. "We've only been married eleven months. She's the prettiest girl in Nevada. Her father was also a sheepman and we sort of grew up with our families. The logging people killed her Pa last year and her Ma went sick and died of a broken heart. Milly feels even stronger than I do about Jeb Oatman and his bunch."

Clint frowned. It was twilight and there was a lingering golden glow on the snow-dusted peaks. This country looked so damned peaceful and serene. But obviously, there was nothing at all peaceful about the situation facing Abner Turner and his bride. Wasn't that the way it always went, though? Wherever the soil was dark and rich, the water sweet and clear, and the grass lush, there was bound to be trouble. Gun trouble.

"Mr. Adams?"

Clint pulled himself out of his dark thoughts. "Yeah?"

"Are you a gun for hire?"

Clint frowned and bit back his irritation. "Do I look like one?"

"Sorta. Yeah, I'd say that you carry that six-shooter on your hip like it was a part of you. Just sort of natural-like. I don't mean to pry or anything, but if you are a gun for hire—"

"I'm not," Clint interrupted sharply. "I'm an ex-lawman and now I fix guns when I need a little spare cash. Sometimes, I earn my living playing poker."

Abner Turner looked sideways at him. "You sure don't look like no gambler."

"That's the reason I'm successful at it. If anyone asks, I tell them I am a good player, but I find that generally makes men want to play me even more. It's more fun to beat someone who figures they're good."

"I can't play cards at all," Turner admitted. "I get sore when I lose a few dollars."

"Then you've no business playing. A man should never gamble more money than he can afford to lose."

"I can't afford to lose anything." Turner pulled his hat off and scratched his scalp. He had thick, long hair that looked as if it had never felt a brush or comb. "But if I sold the homestead, Milly and I would be durned near rich."

"Is that a fact?"

Turner swelled up with pride. "Yessir! You see, it's like I was trying to explain. Our land sits right astraddle the Carson River, and we're the first ranch at the highest part of this valley. That means Milly and I control the water to those ranchers below. It sure galls the cattlemen, but they choke it down. But the other thing that makes our spread so valuable is that we have about three thousand acres of prime timber on the eastern border of our range. That's what the logging companies are after. That, and the right to send their logs downriver without paying me a cent."

"You charge them?"

"A penny for every ten logs," Turner said. "That's cheaper than anyone I ever heard of charging."

"You're right," Clint said. "That sure isn't much money."

Turner laughed outright. "Mr. Adams, you have no idea how many logs come floating down that river from the slopes above our ranch. Why, at certain times of the year, there are thousands. You just saw one lumber mill. There are five more downriver. You ever been up on the Comstock Lode?"

"Yep."

"Well, what you see above ground is nothing compared to what's below ground. Sun Mountain is catacombed with underground tunnels. I've heard that there are so many miles of mine tunnels that if they were stretched out in one line they would reach all the way to the Pacific Ocean."

Clint shook his head. "I don't believe that."

"Neither do I," Turner admitted. "But I can tell you this, those mines under Virginia City, Gold Hill, and Silver City are gobbling up the entire eastern slope forests. All of it from Reno down past Bodie in California. You see, without timber, the mines would have to close down. They got to keep digging new ore and to get to it, they have to leave the old shoring in place."

"That makes sense."

"Sure it does! From their point of view. But what about people like myself who aren't too excited about seeing this whole eastern slope stripped bare? You see, what'll happen is exactly what's happening over in California."

Clint waited. He knew that Abner Turner was going to tell him about California whether he wanted to know or not.

"In California," Turner said, "they got all the easy placer gold out of the streams and rivers. When that was all gone, they started using hydraulic mining to blow away entire mountainsides. I tell you, when a mountainside is stripped of all forest and brush, it's like raw flesh. It just bleeds away and what you have left after a few years is nothing but rock and gravel that won't grow anything."

"You sound like you know dirt and agriculture."

"I do," Turner said. "My father was a good farmer. He was smart enough to realize that livestock and farming can go together if the rights of one respects the rights of the other. You can't overgraze land and you can't overfarm it. The soil will fail you every time. And if these mountainsides are stripped, the soil will be washed away in the spring runoff and the Carson River will become nothing but a gutter of mud."

Clint nodded. It made sense. "Are you the only man in this valley that realizes this?"

"Nope. The Mormons do, but Brigham Young has called them all back to Utah territory and they'll be no help. Hell, when everybody found out about Young's edict, they swarmed in like vultures. Wouldn't pay the Mormons much of anything for their homesteads 'cause they knew they had to leave. Mormons put a curse on this valley for a hundred years."

Clint shook his head. "I never believed in curses."

"If you stay any length of time in Pine Bluff," Turner said darkly, "you might change your mind."

Clint looked back at Duke, who was limping along. "I guess I'll have no choice but to stay a few weeks. My horse isn't going to be fit to ride until that rock bruise heals."

"Tom Pearson is a good blacksmith. He can fix that horse as quick as anyone. Fit him with a pair of shoes that won't ever wear out. He's got a good stable, too. Feeds plenty of quality hay and grain. Charges a fair price."

"Sounds like the kind of man I'm looking for."

Abner Turner wasn't listening. "On the other hand," he said. "Milly and I could use some help on the ranch. We . . . ."

Clint had no intention of working on a sheep ranch. His saddlebags were stuffed with greenbacks and he was seeking rest and relaxation, not the drudgery of working from morning to night.

"Not interested," he said.

"I didn't figure you would be. And I can tell you have no love for farming or sheep."

"How can you tell that?"

"By the look of your hands. And the fact that you never asked any questions about what kind of crops I raise, or the soil and rainfall. Or how many ewes lambed this spring. Or any of that. Fact is, you're just not interested."

"You got that right," Clint said.

"But . . . well, I was just kind of wondering if you might be interested in sort of staying with us and being a . . ."

"A what?" Clint finally asked with impatience.

"A sort of protector."

"Protector?" Clint echoed.

"Yeah. Maybe if you're on my ranch, then Oatman and his kind will steer clear of me and Milly. I could pay you fifty dollars a month and board."

"Still not interested," Clint said in a firm voice that left little doubt as to his feeling about such an idea.

"Why don't you at least spend the night with us and think it over. Milly is going to have a big roast of lamb in the oven. Mashed potatoes and gravy. Fresh green vegetables and hot apple pie."

Clint could feel a big hollowness in his stomach. It would not hurt to spend an evening with the man and his wife.

Besides, Clint was sort of interested in seeing the prettiest girl in Nevada. And apple pie was his favorite. "How far is your spread from town?"

"Just south a few miles. I promise to take you into Pine Bluff first thing tomorrow morning," the young sheepman said with a wide grin. "You won't be sorry. I built an extra bedroom for our first child, if the Lord favors us with children. You can use it tonight."

"All right," Clint said, unable to turn the man down. "You're a hard man to say no to."

Turner nodded. "That's what the logging interests say. And I guess they're right. When I want a thing, I generally work until it's mine. And once I got something good, I'm a bulldog for hanging on to it and never letting it go. No matter what the odds are against me."

Clint glanced at the man's face in the moonlight. Abner Turner's strong face was set with determination, and the Gunsmith knew that the sheepman was thinking about his enemies right here in this beautiful valley, as well as his bride and his land. And maybe he was afraid he was going to have to die for them, but if he was afraid, it did not show.

Clint leaned back on the seat and stared toward the dark shadow of the Sierras just ahead. He had the feeling he was being delivered into something far bigger and more dangerous than he could even imagine.

THREE

The Turner ranch was about what Clint had expected it to be. A log cabin set among pines and surrounded by work sheds, corrals, and a large hay barn. Clint had the impression that a lot of pride was involved in keeping things in good order. When they drove in, two Mexican shepherds waved from the porch of their bunkhouse.

There were also at least six sheepdogs to greet them. Clint had observed sheepdogs many times and they were impressive. He knew that a good sheepdog was almost as valuable among the flock as their masters. They were loyal and fiercely protective of their bleating charges. They would face bear, bobcat, or cougar without hesitation.

"Hello there!" a young woman called out from the cabin. "Supper is getting cold! Hurry up!"

"Be right along, Milly. Set an extra plate."

"I can see that," she said. "Welcome, stranger."

Clint dismounted from the wagon and tipped his Stetson to the lady. "Evenin', ma'am."

Milly disappeared inside. He had not seen her face because it was in shadow, but she had a lively step and a pleasant-sounding voice. He set about helping Turner unhitch the team, then led them into the barn.

"Unsaddle your black and put him in this stall. You can put your saddle right over there by the hay stack, and I'll get the grain."

Clint was more than happy to oblige those orders, and when he got Duke into a clean stall, rubbed down with a gunny sack, then watered and grained, he felt a lot easier about the animal.

"Nice barn," Clint said, studying the spacious interior and the wagons that Turner kept inside.

"Thanks. I helped my grandfather build it a long time ago. We didn't have nails back then, and every stick of it is held together by wooden pegs. Grandfather was a fine carpenter. I think he enjoyed building things more than tending sheep. You'll see a lot of his work in our furniture."

Clint joined everyone at the table. The two Mexicans were named Juan and Miguel Escobar. They were very shy young men and spoke no English. Milly, however, could speak Spanish fluently, and she seemed to have the ability to carry on a two-way conversation in both languages so that they were all talking about the same thing, only in both English and Spanish.

"Mr. Adams, it's a pleasure to have you join us tonight," she told him after they were introduced. "My husband enjoys company and so do I. Life can get to be pretty monotonous day after day when you rarely go anywhere. And you are a man who looks as if he has been everywhere."

Clint was not sure what that meant, but even if she had said he looked like he'd climbed out of hell, it would not have made any difference. Milly Turner was a stunning blonde. She had a heart-shaped face, sparkling blue eyes, and an impishness that indicated a rich sense of humor. And even though she was wearing her husband's baggy clothes, it was easy to see that she was a very well-proportioned woman. Tall, lithe, and graceful.

Clint smiled and took the food that was offered. The roast smelled wonderful, and he was given huge slabs of it along with big ladles of mashed potatoes and gravy.

Milly said, "You look hungry, Mr. Adams. I hope you approve of my cooking."

"If he doesn't," Turner said, "I'd guess he's too much of a gentleman to say so."

"Are you a gentleman, Mr Adams?" Her smile was devilish.

"Nope. But any man who did not like your cooking should be boiled in oil. It's delicious."

Milly was very pleased. "Wait until you taste the pie."

Clint was so hungry that he had seconds of everything, and the pie was just as good as he'd expected. Juan and Miguel excused themselves, and while Milly cleared the table, Clint and Turner settled back to digest.

"Just passing through, Mr. Adams?"

"Yes. My horse threw a shoe and then got a rock bruise, so I might be held up a few weeks."

"I saw your horse when you came in. He's a beauty."

"He is, for a fact," Clint said.

Turner shrugged his shoulders. "I offered him a job, Milly. He refused."

She turned to look at her husband. "I can tell from looking at the gentleman that he's never hoed a weed or sheared a sheep in his whole life. Isn't that the truth, Mr. Adams?"

"Yes, ma'am."

"But you are either a lawman or a bounty hunter. Isn't that true?"

"No," Clint said. "Like I told your husband, I'm a gunsmith. Sometimes a gambler. Mostly though, I just like to travel around, sort of seeing the country, minding my own business, and enjoying myself."

Milly grinned. "Minding your own business. I guess you've just told me to mind my own business. Anyway, we can't. Did Abner tell you what we are up against here?"

"Yes."

"And you still turned down the job?"

Turner blushed. "Milly! Would you leave the man alone? He's our guest!"

Milly smiled and that was all it took to dispel any tension

in the room. "I meant no harm, Abner. I was just hoping we might get some professional help. Heaven knows, the law in Pine Bluff won't do anything in our behalf. Why, Sheriff Ford is on the loggers' payroll! We need some help."

"I can stand up to whatever comes!" Turner said, his temper starting to surface. "My pa. . . ."

"He was shot from ambush," Milly said angrily. "Just like my father." She lowered her voice and came over to her husband. "Abner, you're a good man; strong, brave, and honest. But you're no match for the likes of that new gunfighter Oatman has on his payroll."

"You mean the one named Pickney?"

"Yes. And there are three or four others almost as deadly. I just don't want you killed."

Clint shifted uneasily in his chair. "Mrs. Turner, I never came right out and asked your husband, but maybe you ought to consider selling. He said you'd be nearly rich."

"No!" Milly turned her back on the table and began to bang pots and pans around in her anger and frustration. "This is our land and it always will be. Our parents are buried on these two ranches that we made into one. Abner and I swore to love, honor, and protect each other until death do us part. Well, the same goes with this ranch. No one is going to take it unless it's over our dead bodies."

Clint nodded. Never again would he make such a suggestion to the likes of this stubborn pair of young mules. Sure, holding onto your heritage was important—but not as important as holding onto your life. And if they got a fair price, one that would make them almost wealthy, Clint saw no sense in the Turners hanging onto something that was almost certain to get the young sheepman killed. Clint thought that perhaps this couple must not really be in as much danger as they pretended.

Clint joined the Turners out on the porch for a while and the conversation covered more pleasant things. Turner and his wife talked about their childhood and how they had grown up here in this valley to see one huge wave of Forty-Niners sweep west over the Sierra Nevadas and then, ten years later, an even bigger wave of fortune-hunters race back east over the Sierras to the Comstock Lode.

"I was a miner up there for a year," Turner admitted. "It was hell. The men make good wages—best in the world for underground work—but down hundreds of feet beneath the surface the temperature gets to be over a hundred and twenty degrees. They give men ice, but it doesn't help and the air gets foul with gases and sulphur. A lot of men are buried under Sun Mountain and Six-Mile Canyon. A lot more came up sweaty in winter and caught pneumonia. They died within weeks."

"And you were almost one of them," Milly said with a shudder. "I went right up after you with a buckboard."

Turner nodded. "I was trying to save up enough money to buy you a fine diamond wedding ring and a real honeymoon."

"I don't need a diamond ring to tell me I've got the handsomest man in Nevada for my husband. And as far as a honeymoon goes, I like it just fine right here. I just hope we can live in peace and that the logging interests that rule Pine Bluff and this area will realize we can't be bought or scared off."

Turner nodded and stood up. "I reckon I'll get ready to turn in."

"Me, too," Milly said. She took Clint's hand. "I thank you for listening to our troubles. It wasn't right that you should hear all about them."

"Everyone has troubles, Mrs. Turner. I just figure you'll find a way to get along like all the rest of us."

"Sure we will," she told him. "And I'm glad you liked that apple pie. There's some for you and Abner to take with you on the way to Pine Bluff tomorrow. Perhaps we shall see you in town before you continue on to San Francisco."

"I hope so," Clint told her, meaning it. He could not help but feel a strong attraction to this woman and that caused him to feel guilty. Abner Turner was a brave and good man. Probably a better man than himself because he was sticking in one place, setting down roots and building, instead of just drifting from town to town in search of pretty women and the next promising card game.

Clint waited until the young couple settled in, then he stood up and headed for the barn. He checked on Duke and the gelding seemed as contented as could be. "I got a fine livery stable lined up for you tomorrow night, and we'll be resting for a couple of weeks."

Clint frowned and looked back toward the house. "If those two really are in mortal danger, we might even stay a little bit longer. All depends. I guess I'll probably need to find out a lot more than I want to know about Pine Bluff and the trouble that brews here. I just can't ride off wondering if these two are going to be alive from one month to the next."

Clint untied his bedroll and spread it down in the straw. The Turners had wanted him to sleep in their spare bedroom, but Clint felt more comfortable out here in the barn. It was a good barn and if a sudden rainstorm came up, he would still be dry. Besides, there wasn't such a heavy odor of sheep out here. Just horse.

The Gunsmith crawled into his bedroll and thought about the Turners and how it might be nice to find a wife some day and own a fine ranch like this one. Hopefully, it would not be in such a powder keg of a valley. Maybe Dora was still single and looking for a husband to settle in with. Naw, Clint thought, she was too good-looking to stay single this long. She'd be married. But there were plenty of other women who would marry the Gunsmith if he ever decided that he wanted to settle down.

Hell, he thought, he might even meet his future bride-to-be in San Francisco. They had some beauties there. Clint shut his eyes and thought about San Francisco. He'd cut quite a figure with the money in his saddlebags. Why, he'd probably have to beat the women off with a club.

It was a nice thought and he was settling into sweet dreams when the rifles opened up on the Turner house.

FOUR

The Gunsmith came out of his bedroll fast. He grabbed his six-gun, and dressed only in his longjohns, sprinted toward the barn door where he stopped, then eased around the door to cover the yard.

Riflefire was screaming in from several directions. In the pale moonlight, Clint saw that every window of the Turner's cabin was blasted out and so were those in the bunkhouse. All the dogs were out in the middle of the yard, and they were barking furiously. He could hear the two Mexican sheep herders yelling in Spanish. Suddenly, a big cream-colored sheepdog broke from the pack, and with the hair standing up on its ruff, it bared its teeth and started to attack a shadowy figure.

One of the Mexicans rushed out of the bunkhouse shouting for the dog to come back. But it was too late. At least three rifle slugs riddled the dog, and Clint could see its powerful body jerk each time it was hit. The Gunsmith fired at the rifle flashes and heard a yelp of pain.

The Mexican was caught out in the middle of the yard and died in a volley of bullets as Clint swore helplessly. It was clear that the ranch was completely surrounded and to try and reach the downed man would have been suicidal.

But even as Clint was seething with impotent fury, the door to the ranch house flew open and Abner came flying out with a rifle.

"Get back inside, you idiot!" Clint shouted.

Abner was caught in a hail of lead, but he somehow managed to turn around and head back inside the cabin. Clint saw the heavy door slam shut, and he could imagine that Milly was giving that young fool husband of hers a well-deserved tongue-lashing.

Clint took a deep breath and raced for a water trough. He drew the gunfire from the ranch house, and when he threw himself behind the trough, the bullets were splashing water all over him.

But just as soon as the shooting began, it ended. One minute they were under an all-out attack, the next minute the only thing they could hear was the drumming of hooves down the valley.

Abner came storming out of the cabin with Milly right behind him. They rushed over to the riddled body of the shepherd, and Milly burst into tears. Clint stood up as Juan hurried to his dead brother's side. The Mexican fell to his knees and wept.

"I'll get them all for this," Abner said. "I swear that if it's blood they want shed, some of it shall be theirs."

"No!" Milly cried. "Don't you see that's exactly what they do want? They expect you to come racing into Pine Bluff. That's where they can kill you right in front of everyone. You'll be the example they want to set."

But Abner was beyond reason. He looked down at Miguel's body and then over at the sheepdog's torn body. With a strangled oath, he spun around and headed back into the cabin.

"You've got to help me stop him!" Milly said. "They'll be waiting."

"I can't stop him," Clint said, wishing he was dressed and that he could have gotten a better aim on a few of the murdering bastards who had gunned down the defenseless shepherd.

Milly grabbed his arm. "You must help me. If you can just get him to cool down enough to think clearly. By morning, he'll know that what I'm saying can save his life."

"All right," Clint said. "I'll try."

She hugged his neck. "Thank you!" she said as she turned

and rushed back into the cabin.

Clint left the Mexican with his dead brother. There was nothing that could be done. He couldn't have thought of any consoling words even if he could have delivered them in Spanish. What had happened had been murder, pure and simple. Miguel had been a sacrificial lamb, and it now seemed clear that the Turners had not been exaggerating even a little bit when they said that their lives were in danger.

Clint went back into the barn. He pulled on his shirt, pants, socks, and boots. He reloaded his gun and strapped on his gunbelt. He could hear Abner Turner shouting all the way across the yard, and Milly's pleas that he be reasonable.

The Gunsmith had always been reluctant to involve himself in affairs between a man and his wife, but he liked Abner too much to allow the hot-headed young sheepman to throw his life away needlessly.

Clint stepped outside and waited for Abner to come for his horse. The door slammed and the powerful sheepman had a rifle clenched in his fist when he came marching across the yard.

Clint blocked his path. "I can't let you go off half-cocked like this, Abner. You have a wife and a future to think about. You're a man and that means you have to use your head sometimes and there will never be a better time to start than now."

"I offered you a job. You refused. Get the hell out of my way."

Clint shook his head. "I'll take your offer, but we do this my way."

"Mr. Adams, I never took orders from a hired hand before, and I'll be damned if I'll do it now."

"You don't even know who shot Miguel and your dog."

"Oh, yes, I do! It was Pickney and those others that Oatman hired."

Milly joined them. "But we don't have any proof! Can't you see that?"

Abner lifted his rifle up in front of his chest. "I don't

need proofs and if I wait for it any longer, I'll be as dead as Miguel. Now stand aside!''

Clint took a step backward and drew his six-gun in one swift motion. He pointed it right at Abner's chest and said, "Turn around and march back into your cabin. We'll talk this over, and in the morning, we'll both ride into Pine Bluff and see the sheriff."

"He's on Oatman's payroll! I told you that!"

''Fine,'' Clint said stubbornly. ''Then we'll tell whoever is important in Pine Bluff about this, and that way, at least when trouble comes, we've gone on the record as having tried to get things cleared up legally."

"Listen to him!" Milly pleaded. "For me. For our future children."

Abner swallowed noisily. His face worked with pent-up rage but as each second passed he seemed to gain a little more control of himself. "All right." He gritted his teeth. "But we go into town in the morning and we get some answers."

Clint relaxed. The man was thinking again. "That's right," he said. "We get some answers and we see if we can get some proof. Something for a United States Marshal to use as an arrest warrant."

"You mean, we have to get outside help." Milly was looking right at him.

''That's right.''

To Clint's surprise, Milly shook her head. "It will never happen. You don't understand that all the power and influence, the money that greases the politicians' hands in Carson City is with the logging people. We'll never get a fair deal from the law. And whether you want to admit this or not, we're on our own."

Clint sighed. Milly Turner was probably correct. Clint had been a lawman for a good number of years and most of his peers were honest, courageous men working for damn little pay and respect. Because of that, money and small-town politics quite often got in the way of justice. It was sad, but a reality that the Gunsmith had reluctantly accepted in others. But not for himself.

"Listen," he said, "if this Pickney fellow or some other is the one that killed Miguel, and if we can prove it and get the man sentenced to hang by the neck, would you then consider that justice was done and that you might be better off selling out? There's no point in getting killed, and I can't guarantee that I'll be that much help."

"We don't expect any guarantees from you," Abner said. "In fact, I've decided that there is not a hell of a lot you can do here. This is our fight and we're the ones with our lives at stake. This is our home. We'll not sell it because we were forced to run away."

"After watching you burst out of your cabin, I'd have to say that if you weren't the luckiest man alive, you'd already be dead by now. That was one of the dumbest moves I have ever seen anyone make and survive."

"Well, what the hell was I supposed to do!" Abner raged. "Just lay there in my cabin and watch them murder my men and my dogs!"

"No," Clint said. "But getting yourself killed as well sure as the deuce wasn't the smart thing to do."

Abner bristled. He looked ready to swing that Winchester and flatten Clint, but Milly stepped between them and prevented an almost certain fight. "Stop it, both of you! We've all got to help each other, not fight among ourselves. Look at poor Miguel. If you want to do something so badly, dig his grave while I make some food and talk to poor Juan about his brother."

Abner nodded. "Milly is right."

"You dig Miguel's grave," Clint said. "I'll dig another one close beside it for the dog."

And that was the way they spent the rest of the night.

FIVE

It was a beautiful morning, and Clint might have enjoyed it if they hadn't buried Miguel Escobar at daybreak. It was not the first day that Clint had ever started off with a funeral, and it probably wouldn't be the last. Juan Escobar could not stop weeping, and it was clear that he had worshipped his older brother. Witnessing the young Mexican's grief soured the Gunsmith almost beyond measure. It didn't help any when he glanced over at the ranch and bunkhouses and saw all the broken glass windows.

The sun was climbing steadily when they finally finished up with the burying and got the team hitched to the buckboard.

"I think you and Juan ought to come with us," Abner said to his wife. "They could come back at any time."

But Milly wouldn't hear of that. "I have glass to clean up and work to do around here. Besides, they're cowardly men. Bushwhackers. Their kind shoots from the cover of darkness. They'll not take a chance on being seen."

Clint hoped she was right. It was clear that Milly Turner would not change her mind under any circumstances. "We'll get back as soon as we can. Meanwhile, I think you'd be wise not to leave the ranch. You also need to keep a sharp eye on the dogs. They'll be first to hear or smell anyone."

Milly glanced at the dogs. "I appreciate your concern but I can't stay here with five thousand head of sheep grazing up the road a few miles. They've got to be looked after or we could lose them."

31

Clint frowned. "Better a million woollies than your life, Mrs. Turner. If you have to go, my advice would be to send Juan out to bring the flock in nearer to the ranch."

"Look at him. Does he look fit to do anything more than grieve?"

"No," Clint admitted. The Mexican was almost incoherent in his grief. "I guess he doesn't. But I think . . . ."

"I'll be all right," she said. "Please just go to Pine Bluff and do what has to be done. I promise to take the dogs and a rifle."

Abner climbed up into the wagon and said, "Clint, she's as stubborn as a mule, and a team of wild horses couldn't keep her away from those sheep this morning. Get in and we'll be back before noon."

Clint had no choice but to climb into the wagon despite his misgivings. When the buckboard lurched away from the Turner ranch, Clint stared straight ahead and worried, paying no attention to the soft breeze that blew the scent of pine from the mountains or of the grass that waved like wheat with the shine of sunlight laying easy on each blade.

Yesterday he'd been looking forward to revisiting Pine Bluff on the slim possibility that Dora might still be available. But that was wishful thinking, and had it not been for the fact that he had been fired upon and the ranch attacked by a bunch of murdering sonofabitches, Clint would have liked to have kept traveling. But then there was Duke to think of, so he guessed maybe it was fate that he wasn't going anywhere.

"How good with a gun are you, Clint?"

The Gunsmith shrugged. "Good enough to keep myself alive the last ten-fifteen years."

"You've killed a few men, haven't you."

"More than a few," Clint said quietly. "But I'm not proud of the fact. Those I've killed either deserved it or left me no alternatives."

Abner Turner chewed on that for several minutes. "I wish to God that I'd have learned how to use a gun when I was younger. I'm a good shot with a rifle but a terrible one with a handgun."

"Most farmers, cattlemen and sheepmen are in the same boat you are," Clint said. "A handgun isn't much use except for shooting rattlers and outlaws. But a fella like yourself has all kinds of uses for a rifle—wolves, coyotes, a horse, dog, or ewe that needs to be put out of its misery. Bobcats and hungry mountain lions. But a handgun? Well, that's sort of a specialized weapon. Would you like a piece of advice?"

"As long as it's free."

"All right," Clint said. "If you ever face a professional gunfighter, put some distance between yourself and the man."

"You mean just turn my back and run like a coward."

"Not like a coward, like a man with brains. Like a man who means to turn bad odds or none into good odds that he'll survive. You just turn and get the hell away as fast as you can. A good hundred yards or more before you turn and use that rifle against a six-shooter. Do that and you have a fair chance of winning even against a professional."

Abner thought about that for a while and it was clear that the idea of running was entirely against his nature. But to his credit, he said, "I'll try to remember that because it makes sense."

Clint leaned back against his seat. "Tell me about your sheriff."

Abner snapped the reins down hard on the backs of the team, and they jumped forward to hurry along the road at a fast trot. "Sheriff Doug Ford is a fat, two-faced sonofabitch who takes his money from the highest bidder. He has a deputy named Rangles that is gun-crazy and also into the pockets of the logging companies up on the mountainside. But Jeb Oatman is the big man on the mountain. He's the one behind all of this."

"Tell me about him."

"Not much to say. He's ruthless and started out on a logging crew. He whipped and fought his way up to foreman, then bought into a company and took it over a couple of years ago after his partner mysteriously fell into a logging chute and was crushed."

"Doesn't sound too believable," Clint said.

" 'Course it doesn't. Everybody knew the man was murdered. But there was no proof. Sierra Timber was reasonable back then, but after Oatman took over the reins, they got real greedy and started gobbling up timber rights all over the eastern slope. And those that wouldn't sell either had accidents or were run out of Nevada."

"Does this Oatman have an office in town?"

"Yeah. But I got thrown out of it the last time I tried to beat his brains in. They won't let me past the front door. If they see you with me, they won't let you in, either."

"Then as soon as we have a talk with the sheriff," Clint said, "we'll split up and I'll have a word with the man."

"He'll deny he knows anything about last night."

"Of course he will." Clint's eyes narrowed. "And there is no way for us to prove otherwise."

"Then what—"

"I don't know," Clint said, interrupting the sheepman. "But sometimes, a little warning goes a long, long way."

Abner just shook his head. "Nobody warns Jeb Oatman about anything. He warns them. Oatman has the guns and the power to back up his tall talk."

Clint did not say anything more. Abner didn't know about the Gunsmith's reputation and how it could influence men. But if Oatman had been around even a little, he just might recognize the name Clint Adams, and it was a dead certainty that his gunnies would as well. Clint would have preferred not to have traded on this identity, but in this case, there seemed little or no choice. He could not take the risk that there would be anymore night attacks. And with a little time and some digging around Pine Bluff, the Gunsmith was sure that some evidence against Oatman and his cohorts would surface. Once that happened, he could proceed to telegraph some friends of his in the law profession. Within days, Clint was sure that a United States Marshal would arrive with an arrest warrant.

"Are you famous or something?" Abner asked.

"Naw." Clint shrugged innocently. "I'm just a naturally confident kind of a man."

Abner snorted with disbelief. "You just don't have any idea about what a stacked deck we're up against in Pine Bluff."

"Maybe not," Clint said. "But things have a way of working themselves out right if you have a little faith."

"You are the damnedest, most optimistic fella I have ever come across," Abner said. "But I got a feeling that I'm lucky to have you on my side. After what happened last night, nine out of ten men would have hightailed it down the road quicker than a spit. But you stuck. Milly said you are a special kind of man. Watch out that I don't get jealous."

"You won't have time for that," Clint said. "We'll get this wrapped up in a few days and once I know you and your wife are no longer in danger, I'll be moving into a hotel room in town."

Abner shook his head. "The way you talk, so sure of yourself and everything, I almost can believe that. I can't tell you how much Milly and I just want to be left alone."

"You will be," Clint promised. "Before I ride over those mountains into California, you will be, for a fact."

SIX

Pine Bluff had tripled in size during Clint's absence. It no longer had the look of a forest outpost. Now, there were two hotels, several cafes, at least five saloons, and several other kinds of establishments. The town itself was situated right at the base of the Sierras. There were pine trees all around it and the moment they entered the main street, they were joined by a number of freight wagons loaded with timber and supplies.

"It's sure grown," Clint said. "When I was through here last, it wasn't much more than a sleepy logging town."

"It's the Comstock Lode that's changed everything," Abner said without enthusiasm. "Damned strike has brought hordes of people through here. There are at least a dozen wagons going over Carson and Luther Passes every day. Why, you'll see everything from disassembled mining tanks and equipment to pianos crossing over the Sierras. There's a lot of riffraff passing through as well."

Clint could believe it. Although it was still early in the day, the saloons they passed were filled with loggers, miners, and teamsters. Everywhere the Gunsmith looked, he saw new homes and businesses being constructed out of timber.

"Lumber is almost as valuable as gold in these parts," Abner was saying. "That's why, in addition to my water rights, Jeb Oatman and the rest of the logging companies that he lets compete are after my land."

Clint shook his head. After last night, he was sure ready

37

to believe Abner Turner, but it seemed impossible that anyone could want his timber when there was still so much left in these mountains.

As if reading his mind, Abner said, "Don't be fooled by all the timber you still see on these mountains. Why, it's only standing because Oatman and the rest have figured out that if they control the supply, they control and raise the prices. Besides that, timber far from a river is a hell of a lot more expensive to log than, say, the stuff on our place. With my timber, all they'd have to do would be to chop it down, trim off the branches, and drag it a few hundred yards to the Carson River. Big profits can be made that way."

"I never learned much about the logging industry."

"It's just as well," Abner said. "The men are hard, harder than cowboys, and even harder than miners. And that's saying something. Pretty dangerous work, too. There are at least two or three men killed every week in some accident. Most logging companies don't give a damn about the safety of their workers. Not anymore than they do about stripping the hills and ruining the soil and rivers that feed the valley.

"There's the sheriff's office just up ahead."

The Gunsmith saw it. "Pull up and let me off. I'll have a talk with the man. What did you say his name was?"

"Doug Ford. He's worthless but also nearly harmless. Now Deputy Rangles, he's a different story. Ford puts up with him because of his gun speed. He's killed at least three other gunfighters that I know of. One of them, named Dirk Cork, was supposed to be mighty fast."

"Rangles outdrew Dirk Cork?"

"He did, for a fact."

Clint shook his head. "Dirk Cork was one of the fastest men alive with a gun. I saw him once down in Arizona. He was something."

"Well," Abner said. "I didn't see the gunfight, but I heard two or three men tell about it and their stories were all the same. Rangles challenged Cork—and the man was sober and armed—and then outdrew him cleanly."

"Then I'll have to be wary of that deputy," Clint said, deciding that it served no purpose to tell Abner that he had also outdrawn Cork in Tucson and taken him to jail. He'd beat Cork and managed to wing him in the gun arm, but it had been a pretty close contest. This Rangles fella had to be damned fast.

Clint jumped down from the wagon.

Abner frowned and it was clear that he was not happy. "What am I supposed to do while you're talking to the sheriff and then Oatman?"

"Stay out of trouble. Buy supplies. Visit with your friend the blacksmith. I'll meet you there before noon."

"You don't even know which one is Tom Pearson's livery."

"Sure I do," Clint said, pointing down the street. "It's that one at the far end of town. I can read his sign."

"Damn, you got good eyes!" Abner said, squinting at a sign that no human eye could read from this distance.

Clint smiled. No need in telling the sheepman that he had stopped at Pearson's and boarded Duke the last time he had been through Pine Bluff. The Gunsmith watched Abner drive away, and he was soon swallowed up in the traffic that clogged the streets.

When Clint entered the sheriff's office, his impression was very unfavorable. The office was in a total state of disorder. There were papers an inch deep covering the entire top of the man's desk. Trash was piled in the corners, the rifle case was busted and unlocked, the Wanted posters were so old and outdated as to be yellowed, and worst of all, there was a bottle of whiskey right out in plain view. The last thing that Clint would ever have tolerated as a sheriff was drinking on the job.

Deputy Rangles was in his mid-twenties and dressed like a dandy. His boots were polished and his long black hair was combed straight back and slicked down with grease. He wore a gold watch fob and a scraggly beard but no mustache. He looked as vain as a peacock, but the gun on his hip looked well used. He was looking at an old newspaper and paid Clint no attention when he walked in. That annoyed the Gunsmith, so he moved over to the deputy and said, "You got time to tell me where the hell the sheriff is, or what?"

Rangles didn't even look at him. "You sit down and shut up, Mister. When I'm through reading this here paper, I just might answer your question if you've learned any manners."

Clint swatted the paper in his left hand. Rangles hadn't been expecting anyone to dare to challenge him, but he recovered very quickly. With an oath, he started to come out of his chair, but Clint had him off balance and he wasn't about to lose that advantage. His right hand grabbed the deputy's shirt, and he shoved the man back into his desk chair so hard he almost went over backward.

"Goddam you!" Rangles bellowed, attempting to claw for his six-gun. "I'll . . . ."

Clint had the man cold. His own gun was out of its holster and steady in his fist. Rangles froze. "Who the hell are you?" he whispered, staring at the gun pointed at the space between his eyes.

"It doesn't matter as long as I have this gun pointed, does it?" Clint asked.

Rangles shook his head. "You got the drop on me this time. Be different next."

"If you don't tell me where the sheriff is, there might not be a next time for you," Clint said.

"If you come here to work for Mr. Oatman, say so now, dammit!"

"I'm working for the Turners," Clint said, watching the shock and disbelief build up in the deputy's eyes.

"That could be a real fatal mistake, stranger. Real fatal."

"So could not telling me where to find the sheriff."

"He's over at the Branding Iron Cafe eating his breakfasts. He eats at least two, sometimes three. The man is a swine."

"A deputy ought never speak ill of his boss," Clint said

as he brought the toe of his boot up, catching the edge of the seat and sending Rangles crashing over on his back. The man screamed in anger and, before he could recover, Clint was out the door. He walked ten paces and whirled around, but Rangles did not come for him.

Clint smiled. He hadn't even met the sheriff or Jeb Oatman, but already, he had made himself a real enemy.

Sheriff Doug Ford was easy to pick out among the crowd of breakfast diners. The man was gigantic. He had a smallish, bald head with waddles of fat for a neck that fed into a pair of huge, sloping shoulders. He occupied an entire table all to himself and there really were two complete breakfasts—or what was left of them—in front of him. The sheriff of Pine Bluff was in his late forties and his clothes were stained and crusted with food. The Gunsmith could not help but feel a strong sense of revulsion even before he crossed the room.

"Sheriff Ford, I need to speak to you."

The man looked up at him. He had small, deepset, bloodshot eyes. "See me during office hours."

Clint drew up a chair. "I'll see you right now."

Ford started to bluster, but then he recognized Clint and the bluster died before it was born. "You're the Gunsmith, aren't you?"

"That's right."

The sheriff sat up in his chair and bellowed, "Matty, clear these goddam dishes and bring me and my friend two cups of fresh coffee—on my tab."

"I'm not your friend," Clint said. "As a matter of fact, I'd say we're definately on the opposite side of the fence. I'm working for Abner Turner and his wife. You're on Jeb Oatman's payroll."

The sheriff paled a little and his smallish head began to wag back and forth. "Now wait a minute," he protested. "I'm not on Oatman's payroll. I work for the people of Pine Bluff."

"Sheriff," the Gunsmith snorted. "This size of town can't

pay you what it must cost for that deputy and all the food you eat."

The man blinked and his face grew red. He looked around him and saw that people had overheard the conversation. "I think we had better go over to my office and have a long talk."

"What about the coffee?"

"I'll make up a pot."

"Okay," Clint said. "But I think I'll drink a cup here while you go tell that trigger-happy deputy of yours that he needs to learn something about respect and loyalty."

"Rangles and you crossed swords?"

"Let's just say we didn't part friends."

The sheriff nodded. "I'll bet that stupid sonofabitch didn't even recognize you."

"Just talk to him, Sheriff. Tell him to be nice or stay out of my sight. I'm getting too old and cranky to put up with his kind."

"Did you ever?"

"No," the Gunsmith admitted.

"I'll talk to him. And then, we're going to tell you about the way to get along in Pine Bluff and maybe make some money besides. Interested?"

Clint managed to smile. "Sure," he said, deciding that the best thing to do was to learn what kind of hand the opposition was holding. "Money always talks."

The sheriff relaxed and a broad grin creased his face. "Attaboy! Hell, you're still a pretty young man. There's a lot of money floating around in Pine Bluff. Some of it can be yours. I'm not greedy. You can ask Rangles about that. He does right well."

"Dresses nice."

The sheriff winked. "He thinks he's quite a ladies man. Truth of the matter is, none of the saloon girls want anything to do with him. He says it's because he's hung like a horse, I say it's because he's got a wild and mean streak in him and he likes to hurt the women."

"Is there a saloon girl named Dora still in town?"

The sheriff blinked. "How do you know her?"

"We're old friends."

The sheriff mopped his face with his napkin. "Rangles had her awhile. He still thinks she's his girl. If you see her, there's not a thing that I can do to stop a gunfight."

"Sheriff," Clint said, "if a gunfight is bound to come, then let it happen and we can go from there. Now go tell your deputy to take a walk and let's get down to the facts of life here in Pine Bluff."

Doug Ford hauled his bulk out of his chair. He laid fifty cents down on the table just as the waitress arrived with two coffees. "On me, Honey."

The sheriff dropped an extra two bits on the table and as the waitress turned, he pinched her on the butt. She swung at him but he moved well enough to get out of the way. He was grinning when he went out of the door.

A minute later, the waitress came by and said, "I hate that filthy glutton. You a friend of his?"

"Nope."

"Good," she snapped. "And if I were you, I'd keep it that way."

Clint sipped his coffee and found it strong and to his liking. "I believe I will," he said as he watched the sheriff waddle across the street and disappear into his office. "Yes, Ma'am, I sure will."

SEVEN

As Clint was finishing his coffee, he saw Deputy Rangles emerge from the doorway of the sheriff's office, which was located directly across the street. A moment later, Rangles slammed the door shut and stomped down the boardwalk. It was obvious that he was furious, and Clint had no doubt as to the cause of Rangles' anger. Clint made a mental note of the fact that Deputy Rangles, while he has probably very fast with a gun, had an ungovernable temper. A temper that could be exploited to the Gunsmith's advantage at a critical moment.

"See you later, Matty," Clint said as he left the cafe.

"You can come back any time, just don't bring the sheriff with you."

Clint walked across the street. Deputy Rangles watched him and their eyes locked. It was clear to the Gunsmith that Rangles was itching to challenge him to a gunfight but wasn't quite sure he could win against such a legendary figure. Rangles was the kind of man that would fester inside wondering whether or not he could win the Gunsmith's reputation. The festering would go on until, sooner or later, Rangles would have to find out or go crazy.

"Come on inside," Sheriff Ford said, closing the door behind the Gunsmith and offering him the only other chair. "Coffee?"

"I've had enough," Clint said. "Tell me about Jeb Oatman and how the logging interests run Pine Bluff."

Ford sat down and steepled his pudgy fingers. "You said

you were working for Abner Turner."

"That's right. And you said that was a big mistake."

"It is. Whatever little pissy money Turner is paying you, we can do a whole lot better."

" 'We' meaning you and Oatman?"

Ford nodded. "I sort of run the day-to-day things in town. I keep law and order, and it's not often I have to point my deputy at someone who wants to change things."

Clint leaned back in his chair. "The way Turner explains it, the people doing the changing are those on Oatman's payroll. All he wants to do is just to keep his land."

"Did the man tell you how much Mr. Oatman offered him for this ranch?"

"No."

"Thirty thousand dollars in cash. The fool and his pretty young wife turned it down flat."

"Maybe the timber and water rights are worth that much alone," Clint said.

"They ain't worth anything if you're dead!" Ford sat up straight in his chair and cut wind. "Didn't mean to yell, Gunsmith. Truth of it is, I sort of like Turner and I admire his wife. She could have married some rich sonofabitch, but she chose Abner. They're fine people and I don't want any harm to come to them. But they seem duty-bound to get in the way of progress and mess up things around here."

Clint nodded. "Maybe I could change their minds. If there was something in it for me."

The sheriff grinned. "If you could do that, you'd be doing the Turners a mighty big favor as well as Mr. Oatman and the logging people. Everyboby would come out ahead."

"So why don't you go tell Oatman that I want to have a little talk?"

"Gunsmith, you must have been reading my mind 'cause that's exactly what I was figurin' to do. I know he's tied up in a meeting this morning, but he's almost always free in the afternoon. Why don't you plan on being by his office around three o'clock."

"All right." Clint got up to leave. "By the way," he said, "do you know who attacked the Turner place last night and killed their shepherd?"

The sheriff blinked and his mouth started to open, but he was just clever enough to avoid the trap. "I haven't a clue," he said. "There are a lot of hard cases in this area. Could have been damn near anybody."

"Including your deputy?" It was obvious to Clint that the sheriff himself was too fat to be raiding at night.

"Rangles? Hell, no! He was right here last night until ten o'clock and then he went over to the Double Eagle Saloon."

Dora used to work there. "To see Dora?"

The sheriff shrugged. "Last I heard, they weren't getting along too well anymore. Rangles has been pretty raw over it lately. I suspect he'll find another woman to take Dora's place soon enough. I mean, hell, they all act the same in the dark, don't they?"

Clint got up without answering the man's question or even cracking a smile. "Tell Oatman I'll be around to see him at three o'clock," he said. "Maybe we can help each other."

Ford lumbered after him but stopped at the door. "Mr. Oatman is a real generous man, Gunsmith. He treats his friends right."

"I'll just bet he does," Clint said as he turned and headed for Pearson's Livery.

When he rejoined Abner, Clint met the blacksmith. Tom Pearson even looked the part of a blacksmith. He was tall, square-jawed, and rippling with muscles. His faced was covered with sweat as he turned a cherry-red bar over and over in his forge and then shaped it on his anvil. "Howdy," Pearson said when they were introduced. "Don't I recognize you from somewhere?"

"It's possible," Clint said. "I was through here a few years ago and boarded my horse at your livery."

"That's it, then," Pearson grunted as he pounded away

at the metal bar he was shaping into a horsehoe. "I never forget a face but I never remember a stranger's name. Abner says you were a real help last night."

Clint shrugged. "I was there and did what I could."

Pearson studied the horsehoe and then, apparently not quite satisfied it was hot and therefore malleable enough, he plunged it back into the fiery bowels of the forge and began to pump the bellows. "There's a lot of people in this town that owe their livelihoods to Jeb Oatman and his friends. Me, I won't deal with them. It hurts me in the pocketbook, but I never figured money should come before a man's principles. Abner, well, he and Milly sort of feel the same. I guess maybe you do, too."

"Maybe. Then again," Clint added, "I believe there are times in a man's life when principle should take a back seat to survival. A dead man don't have any principles at all."

The two friends thought about that for a few minutes in silence, which was finally broken when Abner said, "What did the sheriff have to say?"

"He's making me an appointment to see Oatman this afternoon around three o'clock."

Abner frowned. "He'll offer you more money than I could ever pay."

"And maybe I'll accept his offer in order to get some proof on the kind of trouble he's making."

But the blacksmith said, "And maybe you'll be making so much money you'll forget your principles. It's happened before."

Clint curbed the angry reply that came to mind and said, "I was a lawman long enough to have made a pile of money taking bribes. I never did, though. I've seen men like Jeb Oatman rise, and I've seen them fall. Whatever he offers, I'll probably accept in order to get on the inside of what he and some of the other logging companies are up to. But when the time comes to put the man in jail for the murder of Miguel Escobar, I'll do that, too."

Tom Pearson nodded. He wiped his sweaty face with the

back of his sleeve and said, "Just make sure that they don't already have it planned to kill Abner or hurt Milly. Oatman wasn't born yesterday and he won't trust a stranger until the man is under control. With someone like you, that might take awhile."

Clint agreed. He looked at Abner. "I've got to hang around town for another five hours. You want to go back and see how Milly is getting along?"

"I got to help Tom fix the axle on my buckboard. It's cracked and one good bump could snap it in half. So we'll be here when you finish up."

Clint frowned. He would have rather seen the sheepman return to his ranch and wife. But Clint knew better than to voice his worries. Milly was a very capable woman and probably right about not being in danger during the daylight hours. Clint turned on his heel and started back into town.

"Where are you going?" Abner called.

"To the Double Eagle to see an old friend," Clint told them, suddenly realizing that he wanted to visit Dora and see how much she'd changed. "I'll be ready to leave by four and that should give you both plenty of time to have that axle fixed and the team hitched and ready."

Clint set his sights on the saloon, and a smile formed on his lips as he thought about Dora and how they had been so good together once upon a time.

EIGHT

The Double Eagle saloon was the first erected in Pine Bluff. It had started out as a patched tent where its original owner had sold whiskey off a board plank to those that had come searching for wealth on the Comstock Lode. Over the next few years, the trickle of California fortune hunters had become a torrent and the Double Eagle had prospered. The patched tent had become a new tent, then a large new tent and finally a wood building with sawdust floors. It had been enlarged twice and now it was a showpiece with a sixty-foot polished mahogany bar that had been shipped all the way around Cape Horn to San Francisco, and then packed on wagons and assembled in Pine Bluff.

The Double Eagle had a piano, a huge mirror, and some big pictures of buxom, naked nymphs that reminded whiskey-sotted men of their long lost sweethearts. Dora West had been one of the Double Eagle's first dancers, and she had stayed on to become one of its permanent fixtures. She had her own private room on the second floor and she handled the girls. If a girl could really sing and dance, that was all that was required and she was treated with respect. But if she was just cute, couldn't carry a note or remember her right foot from her left, then Dora expected her to service the men with a smile. Most of the girls fell into the latter category.

When the Gunsmith sauntered in the front door of the Double Eagle, Dora was still in bed with blinders on her eyes to keep out the sun, and cotton stuffed in her ears to shut out the neverending roars of laughter, heavy thudding of boots up and down the stairs, giggles of the girls in their little ten-by-ten rooms as they entertained the men, and the constant sound of piano music. When Dora was awake, she never heard all those sounds, she had long since taken them for granted and blocked them out of her conscious mind. But when asleep, she was easily awakened.

At thirty-one, she was considered old for a saloon girl, and yet she had never succumbed to the debauchery that ruined and aged ladies of the night. She drank very little and then only on very special occasions. She ate sensibly and slept from three in the morning until noon. When she awoke, she ordered juice or milk and then dutifully began a series of morning exercises and stretching that she was sure kept her body young and supple. Dora even opened and closed her mouth wide a hundred times in order to avoid the horror of contracting a double chin. Because of these health precautions and her lifestyle, Dora West remained one of the most desired women on the eastern slope of the Sierra Nevada Mountains.

Lately, however, she had begun to wonder if she shouldn't get married. Find a good and a wealthy man and settle down to raise a family. She was not quite respectable, and yet, she held a station above most women. Dora West could attend church without raising too many eyebrows.

Clint stopped once inside the saloon and waited until his eyes adjusted to the dimness. He saw that little had changed inside. The bar was still the showpiece of the establishment and the mirror was still intact, although someone had shot a hole in one corner and taped it together. There were two new nymph pictures on the east wall, and he did not recognize a single face.

The room was crowded despite the earliness of the day, and Clint found himself almost exclusively in the company of logging men. They wore flannel shirts, big lace-up boots, and all but a few were bearded. Clint heard quite a few talking in Scandinavian languages and they were big, blond men with bulging biceps. Turner had been correct when he'd stated that the loggers were a hard-living and physically imposing bunch. The last time the Gunsmith had been in this saloon, most of the customers had been freighters, and a few were cowboys.

"Bartender," the Gunsmith said. "Is Dora still in the second room on the right?"

The man looked up from the glasses he was filling by the process of lining them all up in three rows of six and emptying a bottle over them in a series of quick swoops. "Yeah, but she don't wake up until noon and she never sees anyone before two in the afternoon."

"Thanks. You have any champagne? Good stuff?"

"How good?" the bartender asked.

"Good enough to send over from France."

The man smiled. "Forty dollars a bottle."

"I'll take one," Clint told the man. "Along with two clean glasses."

"Coming right up, sir!" the bartender said with new respect in his voice. "You really think that Miss West will let you in just because you got some fancy wine? She doesn't even drink except for special occasions."

Clint slapped his money down on the bar. "This is one of them, Mister. Now how about the champagne?"

"You bet!" he said, seeing the tip that Clint was offering.

Champagne in hand, the Gunsmith was stopped at the base of the stairs by one of the house bouncers. "Which one of the girls you payin' for?" he asked.

Clint smiled. "I come to pay a visit to an old friend. Miss Dora West."

"She's the deputy's woman if she's any man's at all."

"She belongs to no man and never has," Clint said, his impatience starting to get the best of him.

The bouncer was bull-necked and his nose was fist-busted.

He looked like the kind of a brawler who would gladly take three punches just to land one haymaker. Clint did not even presume he could outpunch the man and so he said, "Miss West is a friend. She'll be happy to see me and she'll even drink some of this expensive champagne. So please, be a good man and step aside."

"Get lost," the bouncer growled. "Or I'll take that bottle and shove it up your butt then twist the cork off and fill you up with bubbles."

Clint groaned. Why was it that nothing came easy? Why was it that he kept running into men like this who wanted to rearrange his anatomy and probably had the means to do it?

The Gunsmith shrugged. "Listen, I can show you a very personal daguerreotype of Dora and me together when I came through last. She's not dressed, but I'll show it to you anyway if you'll let me pass."

"You got a naked picture of Dora West?" The man showed real interest. "Now that, I would like to see."

"Hold the bottle and these glasses and I'll get it out of my wallet," Clint said, shoving the bottle and glasses in his face.

The bouncer took them and Clint reached down as if toward his back pocket. Instead, however, his hand streaked to his gun and it came whipping out of his holster. Before the bouncer could even react, the barrel of Clint's Colt was smashing him across the forehead. The man's eyes crossed and then rolled up into his forehead. Clint just managed to snatch away the precious bottle of French champagne before the man hit the floor. His thick body did not hide the sound of the breaking glasses.

Clint shrugged. Dora would have some nice glasses upstairs. Glasses fit for a real special occasion.

The sound grew louder and more persistent until Dora moaned and covered her ears with her hands. But the knocking at her door would not go away. A drunk. Somehow, some

drunk that was supposed to go to one of the girls had gotten
his door numbers confused and was stupidly pounding on
her door. And the fool would not quit! With his last sem-
blance of reasoning power, he must have deduced that he
had paid for a girl and, by damned, he would have the girl
if he had to woodpecker the rest of the morning away.

"Get lost!" Dora screamed. "Go away!"

But the knocking persisted until, in a rage, she flew out
of bed and stomped over to the door, ripping her blinders
off and totally unconcerned that she was only half-dressed
in her sheer silk nightgown. She grabbed the doorknob and
unlocked it all in one swift motion and when the door swung
open, her fingers were curved and her nails were bent to
mark up some drunken bastard's stupid face.

But Clint caught her wrist and almost before she realized
what was happening, he was crushing her in his arms and
they were tumbling back into the room. Dora thought she
was dreaming. A wonderful dream that she had never given
up on experiencing again. And when the back of her knees
pushed against the bed, she tumbled back happily and her
lips sought those of the Gunsmith.

"If this really is a dream, Clint, don't ruin it by saying
a single word. Just make love to me like I remember. Just
fill me up with you and I'll be happy."

Clint was more than eager to oblige her. He looked down
at the woman and saw that there were a few lines on her
face that had not been there before. But they were nothing
and she looked wonderful. "You haven't changed. If anything, you look even better than I remember," he said noting
how his voice was thick with desire as he set the bottle of
champagne on her bedside table.

Clint unbuckled his gunbelt and hung it on the bedpost.
He took off his shirt and then kicked off his boots and
stockings. He unbuttoned his pants and tore them off. As
he started to remove the last shred of clothing, Dora held
up her hand in a signal to halt.

The Gunsmith blinked. "What's wrong? Change your mind about all this?"

"Not a chance," she told him, "it's just that, before you take off the rest and we get carried away, why don't you close my door so we don't show my girls all my tricks?"

Clint spun around to see two girls standing in the hallway with ear-to-ear grins on their pretty faces. He dashed to the door. "Go back to work," he told them as he slammed the door and yanked off his very last stitch of clothing.

Dora had used the momentary delay to undress as well. Now, she lay on the bed and her lips were parted and her high, firm breasts were rising and falling rapidly in anticipation. She was a tall girl, dark-haired and dark-eyed. She looked French, but she was really part Greek and part Italian. Dora West's last name was unpronounceable. But when she was like this, with her lean, athletic body coiled and hot for lovemaking, who the hell wanted to worry about such matters anyway?

Clint started to push her legs open, but she grabbed his manhood and pulled him forward like a dog on a short leash. Then she rolled into a sitting position and her mouth opened wide and took him inside. Clint groaned and his legs began to shudder almost immediately.

"Somehow, I'd forgotten how really good you were," he panted as his fingers wrapped themselves into her hair.

She worked on him with her lips and tongue until he thought he was going to explode. When he began to lose control of his hips, he pushed her back and fell upon her as if he were a lion about to ravage its prey. Dora opened herself wide and the Gunsmith drove into her with fierce recklessness. But she was wet and slick and when his long, thick penis sank into its hilt, she reached around and grabbed his buttocks and began to buck like an unbroken filly.

Clint laughed deep down in his throat and lost himself in her body. He kept pleasuring her until they were both moaning and their bodies were slamming at each other like wild, crazy things. Then, they came together in an explosion of sweet torment. Just like before, she raked his back and he emptied himself deep inside her with big, drenching torrents of his seed.

It was fast and powerful. Later, they would go slow and make it so good that they would both want to die in shivering ecstasy.

NINE

Clint lay close to Dora, his body spent and still tingling from their lovemaking. His eyes were closed and his heels were propped up on the foot of the bed. Dora sat cross-legged beside him, her arms folded just under her breasts in a way that made them seem even fuller.

"I wish you could stay right here with me," she told him. "You don't know how privileged an offer that is."

"Of course, I do," he said with an easy, contented smile. "I know that any man in town would give at least a couple of fingers for the chance to be your man. That's why I was wondering why you ever let yourself get involved with Deputy Rangles."

At the mention of that man, Dora's cheeks flamed. "I . . . I felt sorry for him."

Clint raised his eyebrows in question. He did not think that anyone would feel pity for such an arrogant man as Rangles appeared to be.

"Well, I did! You see, he's only been in Pine Bluff six months. And shortly after he arrived and was given the job of deputy, he had to face three brothers in a stand-up gunfight. Nobody gave him any chance at all."

"What about the sheriff? Where was he?"

"Out of town." Dora shook her head. "The man is basically a coward. He always seems to be out of town when there's any real trouble. And that day there was plenty. The Wilson brothers were mean and looking for trouble. They shot a man down in the saloon, and they beat the hell out of one of my girls. I was ready to find a gun and go after those three myself."

"But Rangles played hero and won your heart, is that it?"

Dora looked down at her hands. "I guess that's pretty close to the truth of the matter. Rangles killed them when no one else in Pine Bluff either cared or had the guts to stand up and face them. The deputy was wounded and I sort of helped him recover. One thing led to another and the first thing I knew . . ."

Clint smiled and pulled Dora down to him and kissed her lips. "You don't owe me or anyone else any explanation."

"I know," she whispered, "but with you, I feel as if I want to explain. You see, Rangles is a hell of a man. He has this, this sort of idea that he is invincible and always right."

Clint chuckled. "That kind of attitude has gotten a lot of good men planted in Boot Hill before their natural time."

"I realize that. But he's brave and he can be charming."

"And he can also be a real horse's ass," Clint said tightly. "He and I have already decided that we won't be friends. In fact, I sort of think the man will try to kill me before my business is finished in Pine Bluff."

"I thought I was your business," Dora said, pouting a little.

"You are," Clint told her. "I could have ridden through Reno and saved myself about fifty miles of hard riding on the way to San Francisco. But I made a loop south in order to see you again. Trouble was, my horse threw a shoe and I wound up getting a ride from a man named Abner Turner. You know him?"

"Sure, everyone knows Abner. He's a good man. He used to look at me a lot until he made up his mind to wed Milly. But Abner is hotheaded and he's bound and determined to get himself killed. Milly is the one with all the brains between the two."

"That's what I'd about decided," Clint said. "Anyway, last night, their ranch was attacked and one of their Mexican shepherds was murdered. I've decided to stick around and find out who ordered that raid and see that the Turners can keep their ranch."

Dora expelled a deep breath. "Clint, you have no idea of the amount of trouble you're dealing yourself. I'm sure they told you the situation. The logging interests want the Turner Ranch. They need it very badly."

"So I understand. I talked to the sheriff and he's going to set up a meeting between me and this Jeb Oatman this afternoon at three o'clock. Of course, Oatman won't admit that he has anything to do with the killing or the raiding. That's why I might pretend to go to work for the man."

"Oh, Clint! That's almost certain to get you killed. Did anyone tell you that Oatman hires the best gunmen money can buy? Men like Pickney and Elvis Tate. Why, I'm sure that Rangles and Sheriff Ford are also on his payroll."

"Of course they are. When the tallest timber in this town begins to fall, the forest is going to shake for a while. But maybe then we can also save what's worth saving. Turner says that Sierra Timber has plans to strip the entire eastern slope of the Sierras. I'd sort of hate to see that happen."

"It's already happening." Dora stroked Clint's thigh until he got goosebumps. "If you play the kind of game you're thinking about, you'll have more enemies than you have bullets in your gun."

"I know," Clint said. "But a poor shepherd was gunned down last night and I have a bad feeling inside that there will be a lot more dying to come if someone doesn't stop it pretty quick. I might be able to wire a United States Marshal to help."

Dora looked straight into his eyes and shook her head. "No you won't, Clint. You're the kind that will do it all by yourself. But if you need help or a place to hide in town . . . or anything, you know where I live."

Clint nodded and watched her climb on top of him and begin to do wonderful things to arouse him again. He laced his hands behind his head and closed his eyes. He still had a couple of more hours to play with Dora before his meeting with Oatman. And by then, he was going to be the most relaxed man in the West.

He was still thinking that when gunfire erupted in the street below. Clint heard men shouting and then the boom of a Winchester rifle. And in a flash of intuition, he knew that Abner Turner was being run to ground.

Clint flew off the bed in such a hurry that he spilled Dora to the floor.

"What the hell is the matter with you!" she cried.

Clint threw aside the lace curtains and opened the window. He stuck his head outside just in time to see Abner Turner running down the center of the street with a gunman chasing him. Abner stopped not twenty feet below and slammed the butt of his Winchester to his shoulder. He opened fire and his bullet sent the gunman's hat spinning to reveal that the man had a shock of red hair. The gunman was as cool as a glacier. He dropped to one knee, grabbed his pistol in both hands, took careful aim and drilled Abner in the chest.

"No!" Clint shouted, spinning around and jumping over Dora to grab his gun from its place at the foot of the bed.

But before the Clint could fly back to the window, the red-haired gunman had coolly shot Abner twice more in the chest and the sheepman was lying spread-eagled in the street with three bullet holes leaking blood into the dirt.

Clint stared down at the sight and cursed. "You wait right there where you stand!" he shouted at the gunman who had already turned and was walking swiftly away. "Stop, I say!"

Clint fired a warning shot and the gunman threw himself into the dirt, rolled behind a watering trough, and sent two bullets right at Dora's window. The glass shattered, and the Gunsmith was forced to jump back into the room. By the time he reached the window again, the man was up and running and very much out of pistol range.

"Who is he?" Clint shouted.

Dora threw herself at the window. But she was too late because the gunman was already rounding the corner of the street and disappearing from sight. Dora stared down at the bullet holes in Abner Turner's chest. "They finally killed him," she said quietly. "And they did it on Main Street in broad daylight."

Clint grabbed his pants and pulled them on. He dressed quickly, his mind in a state of agitation because, somehow, he should have realized that this town was so corrupted by the logging men and the sheriff's office that no one was safe under any circumstances. He had liked Abner and he was responsible for leaving the young sheepman unprotected.

"Clint," Dora pleaded, "please be careful out there! Oatman has so many gunmen and you don't know which—"

Clint interrupted her in mid-sentence. "The man who shot Abner had red hair. He was medium height and slender. Who fits that description, Dora?"

"Elvis Tate. Oatman's number-two gunfighter behind Pickney."

Clint nodded. Just in the split second that he had seen the red-haired man in action, it was clear that he was a professional killer. No one but a professional would have been that cool under fire from a rifle. Tate really had been at a disadvantage, just as Clint had promised Abner such a man would be if he were at a distance. But what Clint had not added was that a professional gunman, a real veteran, somehow always managed to win even when he was at a disadvantage.

Clint finished dressing and stopped at the door. "You know, Abner remembered the advice I gave him and he tried to use it. Problem was, I thought he was a better shot, and Tate is an expert. Against most gunfighters, I think Abner could have won."

Dora nodded. "The man is dead and I'm sorry. Tell Milly to sell that damned ranch and get out of Nevada before she is killed as well. They'll do it, you know."

"They will try," Clint said. "But if Mrs. Turner won't sell, I'll back her up until either they—or I—go down."

Dora shook her head. "Why? The woman has a choice. Her husband had a choice, too. They were stubborn and stupid!"

Clint paused at the doorway. "Dora," he said finally, "if you don't understand why I have to stay and fight, then I've overestimated you and you don't understand me at all. I'm going."

Clint left her and hurried down the stairs. It wasn't three o'clock yet, but he was going to find Jeb Oatman anyway.

TEN

"Where the hell you think you're going, Gunsmith!"

Clint had just emerged from the Double Eagle when the sharp challenge caught him in mid-stride. He turned to see Deputy Rangles standing about twenty feet down the boardwalk. A cold fury swept through the Gunsmith. "There's a man lying dead in your street with three bullet holes in his chest. I think you ought to be looking for whoever it was that killed him instead of worrying about me."

The deputy's lip curled. "Maybe you shot him from Dora's window. That's where you been the last few hours, isn't it!"

"You're not only jealous, you're stupid," Clint said. "If you want to die now rather than later, make your play. I haven't time to mess with anyone as ignorant as you appear to be."

"Hold it!" Sheriff Ford bellowed. "By God, one killing today is about all I'm going to stand for in my town."

Clint did not take his eyes off the deputy. He was waiting for the man to make his decision, and he wanted him to make it right now. Clint figured this was as good a time as any to find out just how fast the young lawman really was.

But Rangles backed off. "We got witnesses that Turner provoked Elvis Tate into a gunfight."

Clint shook his head. "I kind of thought it might stack up that way. Where did it start?"

"Outside of Mr. Oatman's office. Turner demanded to see him about the Mexican that got shot last night. Mr. Oatman refused to come out and a fight started. Bullets were fired and Turner just faced the wrong man."

"I was watching from upstairs and it was the same as murder!"

Sheriff Ford pushed between them. He was sweating profusely. In a raspy whisper, he said, "My God, man! I told you that Mr. Oatman could set you up real pretty. You're a professional. Use your head and get control of yourself!"

Ford was right, but for all the wrong reasons. Clint knew that he would only get himself killed if he raced over to brace Oatman's gunfighters. He might beat the man called Pickney as well as the red-haired Elvis Tate, but he would not survive the guns of the others. Better to take them one by one when they least expected it until the only ones left were Oatman and his power-hungry timber barons.

Clint turned away and walked over to the body of Abner Turner. He knelt beside the man and said, "You should have stayed at the livery, where I left you. And more importantly, you and that pretty bride of yours should have sold out and lived the easy life somewhere better than Pine Bluff."

Clint heard a shout. He turned just in time to see Tom Pearson, the powerful blacksmith, grab Sheriff Ford and actually hurl the behemoth through the big plate glass window in front of the Double Eagle. Then, Pearson spun around and jumped at Deputy Rangles. Rangles drew his gun and fired and Clint saw the blacksmith stagger. But Tom Pearson's momentum carried him into the much lighter man and his sinewy hands found Rangles' neck. The pair went down and the blacksmith, though badly wounded, began to throttle the deputy and bash his head against the boardwalk as he screamed into his purplish, contorted face.

It took three men to pull Tom Pearson off the deputy and when they did, Rangles was unconscious. "Get a doctor over here!" Clint shouted, as he tried to calm the blacksmith and keep him from going after Sheriff Ford, who lay cut and bleeding in a sea of glass. "Hurry!"

The doctor raced to the sheriff's side and then over to the unconscious Rangles. "At least the neck's not broken," he said. "Get this man on a litter and keep his neck straight. Help the sheriff up as well."

"What about this man!" Clint demanded, motioning toward the blacksmith who had a bullet in his shoulder.

"He's already dead one way or the other," the doctor said, glancing at the blacksmith's shoulder. "Besides, the bullet went completely through the shoulder; he don't need me nearly as much as he needs a fast horse out of town."

Clint understood what the physician was saying. He grabbed the blacksmith and shoved him through the crowd. "Get your best horse and get out of here before they come for you. 'They' meaning either the sheriff or the men who pay him."

Tom Pearson's rage was gone and now his face was etched with pain as he hurried toward his livery. "But what about my place? I can't just—"

"Yes, you can and you will," Clint said. "I'll see that it's taken care of until this is all over. Then come back. But not until then, or you'll wind up planted beside Abner Turner. Understand?"

Pearson nodded. "Yeah, but it was murder pure and simple. They sent Abner a message to come down to see Oatman. He figured maybe you had gone to see the big man early and needed him there for some reason."

"Will the note be on his body?"

"No," Pearson said quietly. "He wadded it up and threw it in the forge. Didn't seem like any reason to keep it. Wasn't even signed."

Clint nodded. The study of graphology was new and most courts weren't ready to convict a man based on a handwriting sample, but it was still an admissible piece of evidence. If Jeb Oatman had written that note, it might have proven valuable in a court of law.

They entered the livery, and Clint took a moment to bind up the man's shoulder. "The doctor was right. The bullet went through muscle and passed out the back. Probably put a hole in your clavicle."

"My what?"

"Never mind," the Gunsmith said impatiently. "When you've been wounded as many times as I have, you learn all sorts of medical terms. Where's your best horse?"

"The big sorrel down in the last stall. Saddle is over there on that rack."

Clint bridled and saddled the sorrel in record speed. He helped the blacksmith mount and then opened the back doors. "You head for Carson City and a doctor."

"Hell, I don't even have any money."

Clint pulled out his wallet. He was carrying about two hundred dollars and the rest of his poker winnings was already safe in the Pine Bluff Bank. He gave Pearson the two hundred. "Stay in Carson City until I wire you that things are over. If a week goes by without hearing from me, get a hold of a United States Marshal in Reno and tell him that Clint Adams needs help in Pine Bluff."

Pearson nodded. "I sure hate to run, but I know I'd just get myself killed for nothing."

"That's right," Clint said. "So go!"

Pearson, bent over and in great pain, slashed the sorrel across the rump and shot out the rear doors of the stable. Clint watched him disappear around a corner and then the Gunsmith expelled a deep sigh. Instead of pleasuring himself with Dora, he should have been down on Main Street watching out for trouble. Now, Abner was dead, Milly was going to be mad at him, and the whole town was in an uproar.

Clint walked over to Duke and bridled the animal. He brushed him very quickly, deciding that it was pointless to see Jeb Oatman and attempt some pretense at joining his men. The word would already have gotten out that Clint had befriended the blacksmith and helped him escape jail and prison for assaulting officers of the law.

"Duke," he said, "I guess I'll tie you to the buckboard and load up poor Abner's body. I sure ain't looking forward to telling his widow what happened. No sir, I think I'd rather take a beating than do that."

The distinctive click of a gun's hammer being drawn back froze Clint in his tracks. "Move," a soft voice said, "and you're a dead man, Gunsmith."

Clint had no intention of moving. He could just feel that he was now outnumbered in the livery barn, and these men sure hadn't come to invite him to a birthday party.

"Turn around slow."

Clint turned and the next thing he knew, he was lying on his back with his ears ringing and the taste of blood in his mouth. The entire lower half of his face was numb but he knew his lips were already smashed.

"Get up!" the red-haired man said as he adjusted the brass knuckles on his right hand.

Clint discovered that his legs did not want to operate properly. It took him longer than it should have to climb unsteadily to his feet. And when he was up, two big men grabbed his arms and bent them around behind his back while Abner Turner's murderer drove his fists in Clint's stomach three times. Each blow was a sweeping uppercut that completely lifted Clint off the ground. The Gunsmith momentarily blacked out. He awoke when a bucket of water was hurled into his face. Someone grabbed his hair and bent his head back.

"Uh-uh," a voice said. "You're not going to sleep yet. Not until after you talk to Mr. Oatman."

Clint could barely hold his head upright. His lips were smashed, and he was pretty sure that at least one of his ribs had been broken. In a voice he did not even recognize, the Gunsmith choked on a mouthful of blood and managed to say, "Then bring the sonofabitch on!"

Elvis Tate hit him once more in the face, and Clint crashed into a world of spinning darkness.

ELEVEN

Clint awoke to find himself lying in the back of the Turner buckboard beside Abner's body. A man shook him awake and said, "If you have the sense God gave a gnat, you'll help Mrs. Turner bury her man and then pack her things."

Clint barely understood. The man dropped Clint's head down on the hard bed of the wagon and someone slashed the two-horse team across the rump and sent it trotting down the road. The horses knew the way home, and Clint did not have the strength to do anything more than watch Duke's head bobbing up and down as the gelding trotted behind the wagon.

But pride made the Gunsmith sit up before they crossed onto the Turner ranch. With his chest feeling as if it had been caved in by a landslide and his face battered and coated with blood, Clint crawled up into the buckboard's seat and found that the reins were tied to the wagonbed. He untied them and drove ahead until he came to a stream where he steered the team off to the side of the dirt road. He tumbled out of the buckboard and crawled to the water's edge where he buried his face in the cool stream. The chill water, fresh off the Sierra snowpack, revived him almost immediately. Clint washed the blood from his face and peeled out of his shirt. He inspected the purplish bruises on his chest and his flat belly.

Sitting up and combing his hair back with his fingers, he said to himself, "They are going to rue this day. I swear they will!"

71

Clint slowly pushed himself to his feet and staggered back over to the buckboard. He climbed in but not without great effort and no small amount of pain. There were at least two ribs cracked and he knew that they would take a few weeks to heal.

Taking the reins, he gave the team a halfhearted whack across the rump and continued on. They had taken his six-gun but there was another in his saddlebag and his rifle was still tucked under his leg nestled in its worn scabbard. Clint guessed that Jeb Oatman, a man he still had yet to lay eyes upon, and his boys had just assumed that an ex-lawman of Clint's stature would have more sense than to remain where his health was in grave danger. They'd probably figured that a few broken ribs and a busted mouth would discourage anyone with brains from remaining in the area. Well, Clint thought, they have made the serious mistake of assuming I'm an intelligent man. A prudent man who values his life more than his word or his honor.

It was going to be a war. Call it a timber war, or one fought over water rights or just the rights of the little guy over the big one. Call it whatever you chose, but it was going to be a war.

The Mexican, Juan Escobar, saw the wagon first, or maybe it was his dogs and they alerted him that something was wrong. But at any rate, while Clint was still a good mile from the house, both the Mexican shepherd and Milly Turner were running up the dirt road to his aid.

One look at his battered, swollen face seemed to tell the story, and Milly screamed even before she saw the body of her husband resting in the bed of the wagon.

Seeing her face, seeing the grief and anguish, made Clint just want to shrivel up and roll across the Nevada prairie like a dried out old tumbleweed. "I'm so sorry," he mumbled thickly, hanging his head as he stopped the wagon.

Milly Turner touched her husband's face. "When you left, he was worried to death about me and Juan. But I was just as worried about him, and I knew that I should not let him go into Pine Bluff. I knew that they had just been waiting for him to come to town. That's why they attacked the ranch last night. To draw him into their trap."

"He said he was going to stay at the livery and help Tom Pearson fix the axle on this wagon. He changed his mind."

She looked straight into Clint's eyes. "And where were you?"

Clint climbed heavily down from the wagon. "I was where I shouldn't have been," he admitted. "Just like your husband was. Where do you want him buried, Mrs. Turner? Same place as we buried the Mexican this morning?"

"Yes." Clint followed her gaze to the spot. It was on a small, grassy knoll near the stump of an old cottonwood tree. "That's where all the family is buried."

Looking at her, Clint said, "We could . . . well, we could lay him out in your room and wait the night. Bury him in the morning like we did your shepherd."

"No!" She lowered her voice. "Let's get it done right now. Let's do all our burying today and no more in the time to come. I want it finished!"

Clint nodded.

Milly turned to her shepherd and said, "Juan?"

"Si, señora."

She spoke in rapid Spanish and the shepherd nodded. His eyes were swollen from crying and he looked pathetic and beaten as he climbed up into the buckboard and took the reins to drive the team to the burying place.

"You look like hell," she said. "Go to the cabin and lie down. When the burying is over, I'll come in and cook you up something to eat."

"I'm not hungry," he said.

"Well, you look hungry!" She knotted up her fists and then, without warning, she threw herself against Clint and began to pummel his chest. Not hard, not with all her strength, but in a wild frenzy that brought a rush of tears.

"Go ahead and hit me as hard as you can," Clint said in a quiet voice, "I deserve it for letting this happen."

But instead, Milly Turner sagged against him and cried.

● ● ●

Clint did not go to the cabin to rest and wait. He stood beside the fresh grave of Miguel while the young Mexican dug a grave for Abner. He and Milly lowered the man down, and then Milly read a passage from the Good Book before she nodded and the Mexican began to shovel in dirt. He was crying again, and it struck Clint that the shepherds had loved Abner Turner.

Sunset was falling and when a rough wooden cross was placed at the head of the fresh mound, Milly fell to her knees and prayed. Clint stood and waited just out of earshot. He listened to a coyote howl mournfully and it suited the mood. He waited until long after dark and when the widow climbed unsteadily to her feet, he went to help her back to the cabin.

Once inside, she seemed desperately eager to keep busy. She built a fire and made stew and coffee. Clint finally shook his head to indicate that she ought to sit and rest.

"I can't rest," she told him. "Not with what's happened and what is likely to happen next."

Milly studied her hands for a minute and then, almost as if she had an afterthought, said, "Who shot my husband?"

"A man named Elvis Tate," he replied. "Same one that beat the hell out of me, with a pair of brass knuckles. He's the very first man I figure to visit next time I go to Pine Bluff."

"How did they do it so it looked as if it wasn't murder?"

Clint told her. Her expression did not change during the telling.

"What about Jeb Oatman?"

"I never even got to see him. But he's the second man I'll pay a visit to."

"They won't let you get within a hundred yards of his office now that this has happened. I don't even understand why they let you live."

Clint shook his head. "It was their first and biggest mistake," he said, watching the woman closely. "I don't suppose I could talk you into driving your sheep down south a ways and staying there until all this is finished."

"Not a chance."

Clint frowned. "I didn't think you'd go for it."

The woman added, "Besides that, Juan is leaving for Mexico in the morning."

This news did not surprise the Gunsmith. The boy was devastated and since there was a good chance that he might be ambushed, his decision was a good one. "So who watches the flocks?" Clint asked, knowing the answer.

"I will. But there's enough feed on our own range to carry them a few more weeks. I'll keep them close until you're healed and can ride. Clint?"

"Yeah?"

"I was wrong out there to start beating on you like that. It was just that something sort of snapped when I saw the body of my husband lying there. He was a fine man. I guess he might even have sold out if I'd been agreeable to the idea. I feel responsible for his death. I made him think that it was worth dying for what we believe."

"It is worth dying for our beliefs. That's why we live in a free country. And that's why I'm not riding on to San Francisco as soon as my horse and I get healed up."

Milly dished out the stew when it was hot. They both made a show of trying to eat but they did not fool each other even a little bit. When the dishes were washed and the fire died down, Clint pushed himself up from the table and headed for the door.

"Where are you going!" she asked, alarm in her voice.

"Out to the barn to sleep."

But Milly shook her head. "Please," she begged. "Don't do that. I don't want to be alone tonight. Sleep in the guest bedroom."

It wasn't proper, but Clint could see that "proper" didn't mean anything anymore. Not with a band of murderers collected just over the hill in Pine Bluff. "All right."

She actually smiled with relief. "Good night."

Clint watched her go into her bedroom and close the door.

As soon as it was shut he heard her groan and then the sobbing began once more. The Gunsmith stepped outside and glared up at the cold, unforgiving stars. He hobbled painfully across the yard and went into the barn where he made sure that Duke was settled in for the night.

Satisfied, he finally hobbled back to the log cabin. It was quiet and he hoped that Milly Turner had fallen asleep though he suspected she had not. The Gunsmith went into the spare bedroom. The one that Abner had built for the day when he and his wife would have a child.

Clint found the bed comfortable, but his ribs were throbbing and there was a hot bed of anger in his gut that burned. He doubted that Milly would get much rest tonight, and neither would he. For at least a week, he would have to take it easy and let his ribs mend.

But soon enough the day would come when he would ride back into Pine Bluff, and his six-gun would be resting damn loose in its holster.

TWELVE

Milly Turner knew she was more stubborn than brave. She had been raised as an only child and taught that the only way in the world a person could survive was to be strong enough to stand up for their own rights. Well, she and Abner had done just that and what had it gotten them? Abner was dead and so was an innocent young Mexican shepherd who had never harmed a soul in his entire life. And what about Clint Adams? He had been terribly beaten and would no doubt be killed the next time he came across the killers in Pine Bluff.

Milly knew that she could not let that happen. She believed that she had the obligation of stopping Jeb Oatman and exacting justice on Elvis Tate. And justice in Pine Bluff meant killing them like they had killed Miguel and Abner.

Milly thought about that most of the night. She was frightened, lonely and filled with a sense of doom. Her life no longer seemed important—vengeance alone mattered.

An hour before dawn, Milly arose fully dressed and changed into her riding habit. She went to her late husband's gun rack and selected a derringer and a long bowie knife. There was a six-gun in the drawer but she decided that it would be more of a liability than an asset. If she could get close enough to Jeb Oatman, the derringer or the knife would do its work. A big six-shooter would be too obvious and would warn her enemies of her intentions.

Milly tiptoed out of the house and walked across the dark ranch yard. She stopped at the bunkhouse and knocked.

When Juan fearfully asked who was there, she told him to wake up and help her saddle a pair of horses. One for herself, and one for him to ride south upon before anyone came looking for trouble.

Juan joined her in the barn and they saddled the horses. And though Milly did not tell the Mexican of her plans, he seemed to understand what she intended to do. He was very upset. He tried to talk her into leaving with him. Perhaps she could find peace and happiness in Mexico. Juan promised her that his own family would help her, just as she and Señor Turner had helped him and his poor brother.

The offer touched Milly deeply, but she refused. "You must return home to care for your family. Take an extra horse and saddle if you wish and just before you leave, you must wake the man inside and tell him to leave at once. There will be big trouble tomorrow."

Juan's agitation increased when the young woman's derringer accidently slipped from her pocket and fell to the barn floor. He saw her blow the dirt from the little gun and push it deep into her pocket. He shook his head in anguish for he was sure that Señora Turner would be dead before the sun was straight overhead.

"Adios," she told him softly as she mounted her horse in the darkness and rode toward Pine Bluff.

"Adios, señora," he whispered as she rode away. He watched her dark silhouette until it rose over a black hill and then seemed to sink into the earth. Juan made the sign of the cross and set about preparing for his long journey south. He and his brother had saved their money, and he would take it back to Mexico where it would help support his large family.

Juan knew he would not accept the gift of the second horse and saddle offered in kindness by the señora. This would be wrong. The Turners had paid him and his brother very well and to take advantage in such a bad time would be unforgivable. So he gathered the things he had already packed that belonged only to himself and Miguel and then he tied them into a tarpaulin and lashed that behind the cantle of his saddle.

The sheepdogs watched, and they seemed to understand that he was leaving them. They whined softly as if to ask, "But what of our sheep? What of the flock that we were bred to protect with our lives?"

Juan could not bear to listen to the dogs. He chastised them for their whining and they lowered their heads and looked up at him with sad and confused expressions.

When sunrise came, Juan was ready to leave. His horse was saddled, everything was ready. But out on the range he could hear the sheep bleating, and he found he could not quite muster the courage it took to go inside the cabin and wake the hombre who had been so badly beaten yesterday.

So Juan set down on the front porch of the cabin and placed his head in his hands and waited for the man to arise by himself. He would tell him about the señora's decision and then he would have fulfilled his responsibilities. Then, he could finally head for far-away Mexico and home.

Milly reached Pine Bluff shortly after seven o'clock. She rode straight to her lawyer's office and banged on his front door. Miles Ebert was a soft-spoken man of about fifty and he was not surprised to see her. "Come in," he said. "I want to extend my deepest condolences over the death of your husband. You know I was his friend."

"Thank you. Can anything be done to see that the murderer is tried, convicted, and sentenced to hang?"

"Let's not discuss this at my doorstep. Come into my study," Ebert said.

Milly followed him down a narrow hallway into a small office and library. Miles Ebert would not work for the logging industry, so he had not prospered. His clients were exclusively ranchers and a few small farmers. Milly had often wondered how the man paid his bills.

"Please sit down, Milly."

"If I sit down, I might not be able to get up again. Please answer my question."

"All right. The answer is no, there is no way that we can receive justice. I've already inquired and there are several paid witnesses who will testify that Elvis Tate acted in self-defense."

"You know that's preposterous!"

"Of course I do. But their testimony will stand in a court of law."

"But there must have been dozens of people who saw the fight!"

"Your husband sent a bullet through Tate's Stetson. They saw him fire the first shot. The hat itself is proof of the fact. What else is needed to get Tate off?"

"Nothing, I suppose," she said bitterly. "Never mind that then. I have something else I need your help on."

"Don't you think it can wait? My gosh, Milly, it's been less than twenty-four hours since your husband was shot down. And as for the existing will you and your husband had me draft a few months back, you must remember that everything goes to the surviving spouse. Abner made that very clear."

"I'm not here about that," she said. "I want to add something to my will that says, in the event of my death, the Turner ranch will be given to the Territory of Nevada to do with what it will so long as they keep the timber stands from being cut for at least fifty years and agree to double the rate of floating logs across the property."

Miles Ebert blinked at her. "That's a very unusual request. I'm not sure—"

Milly interrupted. "And if the Territory will not agree to this, then I want the ranch to be sold to the Brothers and Sisters of Charity Foundation in Reno for one dollar on the similar condition that they keep it in trust for fifty years."

Ebert nodded with sudden understanding, and it was clear that he approved. "I see. Anything to keep it away from

Sierra Timber or some other logging company's hands."

"Yes."

The lawyer frowned. "Why don't you just sell it to some wealthy cattleman? A man rich and powerful enough to stand up to logging."

"Because I don't know of anyone like that," Milly said. "And anyway, there isn't time."

"Are you sure? You could sell your sheep and—"

"Please! Just do as I've asked."

Ebert was stung but he recovered quickly. "Of course. I'll have the papers drawn up this afternoon and then—"

"No," Milly said. "I need them drawn up for my signature right now."

"As your lawyer, may I ask why?"

"No."

"Then as your friend?"

Milly shook her head. "I'm sorry, Miles. This is something that I can't discuss. I only want you to add what I have just related into the body of the will."

The lawyer studied her face. "I hope you aren't planning to do something rash and maybe even fatal."

Milly forced a laugh that did not sound right. "Miles," she said, "I am all right. Abner and I knew this could happen. I just want to make sure that, in the event of my death, my property is disposed of according to my wishes and those of my husband."

"Very well. If you'd care to browse through my library or just close your eyes and relax, it will only take a short while to make the changes and deletions necessary to put things in order."

Milly touched his cheek. Miles was a scholarly kind of man and a lifelong bachelor. His library reflected his tastes. Dry, academic and very cerebral. He was exactly the opposite of her late husband. Not that Abner had been dull or boorish, for that wasn't the case. But Abner had not been a learned man, and he never read except livestock reports and an occasional newspaper.

"I think I'll just rest my eyes," Milly said, sinking into an old, leather-covered chair. "Wake me as soon as the document is ready for my signature."

Milly sat back and closed her eyes. They stung and she knew that they were red and angry-looking. She wondered how Jeb Oatman's and Elvis Tate's eyes would look when she pointed her two-shot derringer in their faces and pulled the trigger.

THIRTEEN

When the changes in her will were signed and notarized by Miles Ebert, Milly was ready to go. It was still very early and she knew that Jeb Oatman would not arrive at this office for at least another hour, but she would need that time in order to find a way to get close enough to shoot him.

"Milly?"

She turned to face the lawyer as she was about to leave. Ebert's face was lined with worry. "I don't know what you are thinking, but please stay away from those people. You know that they'd shoot a woman as quick as a man."

"I realize that. But listen, what happens if I disappeared?"

"What kind of question is that!"

Milly smiled disarmingly. "I mean if I went on an extended vacation for a while."

Ebert relaxed at once. "Oh. That would be a fine idea. But what about your flock and the Mexicans?"

"I can sell the flock and one of the Mexicans was shot the night before last. The other has left for home."

"I see. Well," the lawyer mused. "If you just decided to vanish until all of this trouble ends, that would be fine. Just let me know what your intentions are."

"I'll do that." Milly figured she had little or no chance of killing her husband's murderer and Jeb Oatman, and still escape with her life. But if that should happen, she had decided that she might make a run for it. Go someplace far away and then come back in a few years and face whatever consequences might still await. But that's wistful dreaming, she thought. The best I can hope for is to kill them before they kill me.

"Good-bye, Miles. And thank you."

He reached out and took her hand. "I have a bad feeling inside. I wish. . . ."

Milly touched his lips with her fingers and his words ended in silence. "I wish you'd find a nice old maid to keep your house up. It really does need dusting," she said, teasing him with the same old joke she and Abner had used so many times before.

The joke, as always, brought a smile to his mouth and that was the way she left him.

Milly made sure that the bowie knife was up her lace sleeve and the derringer was in her waistband. She knew that she would have only one chance at this and she was determined to do her best to rid the world of such vermin as Oatman and Tate.

It was just about eight in the morning when she rounded the corner of B Street and headed straight for the offices of Sierra Timber. Her heels sounded very loud along the boardwalk, and there were few people up and moving around, mostly shopkeepers. Some just nodded or turned their faces as Milly passed, others, like the barber, Ken Howell, were kind enough to stop her for moment to extend their condolences.

"I'm awful sorry about your husband, Mrs. Turner. It was a real shame it had to end the way it did. I guess that he musta went crazy trying to outgun a man like Elvis Tate. He'd a done no better with Pickney. Whatcha gonna do with that big ranch of yours? You could sell out and be durned near rich. A woman alone needs money worse'n a man. But. . . ."

Milly just walked on, not hearing the barber. She supposed there was a lot of talk going around and most of it centered on the fact that, without a man, she was as good as finished. Milly wondered what they would all think when they learned that she had killed Oatman and Tate. Too bad she would probably not be around to hear that gossip!

She rounded a corner and was thinking about this and trying to keep a rein on her rising excitement when, suddenly, a man jumped out between two buildings as she was passing. Milly had just a split second of warning as she saw the gun in his fist come slashing down at her. A cry filled her throat as she recognized Elvis Tate. He was grinning and when he yanked her into the shadowed canyon between the buildings, Milly felt his hands all over her. She was filled with such revulsion that she fought him like a wildcat. She reached for the derringer but it was knocked away, spinning. He had her around the neck and she managed to get the bowie knife out. He was behind her, choking her, and the very best she could do was to drive the blade of her knife back into his body. He howled and let go, but she knew that she had only hit him in the ribs and that there had not been nearly enough force in her stabbing motion to do any real damage.

But the pain must have been great for it caused him to momentarily release her. Milly lunged back toward the street, but he tackled her and when she screamed, he struck her in the face. She felt her body go numb and the scream died in her throat.

Elvis Tate bent down and cuffed the unconscious woman hard. He reached for his side and felt his own warm blood. For a blinding instant, he almost broke the Turner woman's pretty neck, and then he realized that would be a serious mistake. Jeb Oatman would want to decide her fate.

Elvis took the woman's slender neck in both of his hands and pushed his thumbs into the base of her smooth throat. It would be so damned easy just to snap the neck. He had done it several times before with men, hell, with a woman it would be like breaking a stick of peppermint candy.

But reason told him to spare her life. Elvis had always wanted to work for a man like Jeb Oatman; one with lots of money who wasn't miserly. He had been a bounty hunter and an outlaw himself and both occupations were short on pay and long on danger. Compared to some of the scrapes he had squeezed out of, working for Oatman and the logging companies was downright boring. Why hell, yesterday's killing of Abner Turner had been the first real work he had done in months.

Elvis slowly removed his hands from the woman's throat. He stroked the soft mounds of her breasts, and he wished he could spare the time to use this woman for his pleasure. He wouldn't mind doing it right here in the dirt of this alley but if she woke up and started screaming, he might just have to kill her rather than risk the chance that she would tell Oatman what he had done. The boss was funny that way. He didn't bat an eye about killing a man, but he sure held young pretty women in high regard. And Pickney was always looking for a way to put himself above the other hired guns on the payroll. Yeah, Pickney would love it if I screwed this girl and the boss found out, Elvis thought.

Elvis could feel himself stiffening with desire so he took his hands off the unconscious woman before he lost control and didn't give a damn about Oatman or anyone else. A woman as handsome as this could make a man go crazy— even if she was knocked out cold.

Elvis picked the girl up in his arms and carried her deeper into the alley. It had been a real stroke of luck that he had been on his way to the office for an early meeting with Mr. Oatman, Pickney and some of the other men. Just wait until they saw him bring this woman in and throw her down on the floor. Shit, their damn eyes would bug out like a squashed frog's. It was going to be worth something when they realized what he had done.

It might be worth a lot.

FOURTEEN

Elvis shoved open the rear door of the Sierra Timber company offices and stared at the assembly of loggers and hired guns. His eyes found Jeb Oatman down at the head of the long table, and Elvis said loud enough for everyone to hear, "Boss, I brought you a little surprise."

The conversation fizzled into silence. Elvis discovered that he was sweating under his coat, but he had made his entrance and there was no backing out now.

The man at the head of the table leaned forward. He wore a closely cropped black beard and mustache and his eyes were so bright they almost seemed to glitter. Jeb Oatman was thirty-seven, but when you looked deeply into those steely eyes you felt that he might even be older than Cain. He was of average size, but somehow gave the impression of being very large and threatening, because he had a bullet-shaped skull that rested on a massive trunk of a neck. Next to the eyes, when you looked at Jeb Oatman, you were drawn to the jagged knife scar that ran down from his forehead to the base of his ear. The knife had sliced off the bottom of his left earlobe but his hair hid the disfiguration. His nose was long and hooked and his mouth wide and very thin. He looked dead earnest even when seeming to take his pleasure but, in fact, he never took pleasure in anything except women.

"Don't fuck around with me, Elvis. You got something to show, show it!"

"Yessir!" Elvis ducked back into the rear alley and

grabbed the unconscious Turner woman. He had already begun to think that he might be making a serious mistake. But then, what choice had he at the time? The Turner woman had been heading for these offices and, with a bowie knife hidden up her sleeve, it had not taken any swami to figure out what she had intended to do.

"I caught her a while ago," Elvis said quickly as he dragged Milly Turner into the room and watched the surprised looks of everyone except Oatman. "She was coming to kill you, sir."

Oatman stood up slowly, hands on the table. "I may decide to have you killed right now, you stupid, bungling imbecile!"

"But. . . ." Elvis could not believe that his boss had understood what he was trying to tell the man. "But she had a hidden derringer and a bowie knife up her sleeve. Look!" he cried, pulling back his coat to show his own blood-stained shirt. "She almost gutted me. I tell you, she. . . ." Something in Oatman's eyes made his words dribble off to nothing.

Oatman came around the table and everyone parted as he stepped up to Elvis and then slowly raised his hand and slapped the red-haired gunman. Once, hard enough to rock him back on his heels, then a second time so that blood trickled from the corner of his mouth.

Elvis stepped back and his hand instinctively moved toward the gun on his hip. But then, he heard Pickney yell, "Out of the way, Boss, I'll put a bullet through his heart."

Elvis almost fouled his pants. Gun half out of his holster, he froze in fear. His hand released the butt of his gun and flew away from his side. "I didn't have no choice," he stammered. "I swear she was coming to kill you."

"Maybe," Oatman said. "But my guess is that she was going to kill you first. Did anyone else see you?"

"No, sir! I swear I grabbed her so sudden-like that she didn't even have time to scream."

Oatman turned on his heel and marched back to his place

at the head of the table. He looked at the ten or eleven men in the room. Some were his so-called competitors, some were paid gunmen and then there was Sheriff Doug Ford.

"Well," Oatman said to them all, "do I hear any suggestions?"

"Better kill her," Pickney hissed. "No choice."

"And if I did that," Oatman said, turning to his top gunman, "what would happen to the Turner ranch?"

Pickney shrugged. He was a tall, hatchet-faced man in his mid-twenties with a Texas drawl. Everyone feared him and he liked the feeling of being held in awe. "We just take the ranch over. Hell, there's not anyone there except—"

"It doesn't work that way anymore," Oatman growled. "That ranch is the key to the entire valley. Hell, the little ranchers and farmers downriver would scream to the Nevada politicians in Carson City so loud that they'd have to take some action. And there's also the matter of a recorded deed and a will."

Pickney was not a man easily discouraged. "Their lawyer friend, Miles Ebert, he'd be the one who'd have written up anything legal. We could pay him a little visit."

Oatman nodded. "I've already considered that possibility. But Ebert is too smart to leave important documents like wills and deeds in his office. They'll be on record in Carson City. We can't help that. The thing of it is, we have to make Mrs. Turner decide to sell out to us and void her last will and testament."

Oatman returned his attention to Elvis Tate. "All right, as far as she is concerned, I never saw her and I never had anything to do with what you do with her. I want you to take her up into the mountains. Find a cabin where you won't be bothered and get her to sell her ranch with its timber and water rights. Make it damn clear that, if she doesn't cooperate, she'll be fish food at the bottom of Lake Tahoe. I've tried to be fair with the Turners, but they had to do everything the hard way. Take a couple of the boys and don't touch her! At the same time, make things so tough for her that she'll finally agree to sell. When she's ready to deal, send a man down and I'll get a lawyer up there with the papers to sign. I want a signature within one week."

Elvis nodded. One week ought to be plenty of time. "Don't you want to know where we'll be? How about the—"

"Shut up!" Oatman shouted. "I don't want to know, and I don't want anyone else except the men you pick to know. That way, I got nothing to hide."

Elvis Tate nodded. He pointed to three gunmen and said, "Find some rope and tie her up, wrists and ankles. Blindfold and gag her. Phil, you go buy us a week's worth of supplies and Hank, you bring a wagon around to the alley. Make sure you got a tarp to put over her so we can get out of here without her being seen. Race, you make sure we got some good horses and plenty of ammunition."

Elvis bent down and he picked up Milly Turner and heaved her over his shoulder. "Don't worry about anything, Boss. She'll sign."

"As soon as she does, you can use her and then get rid of her."

"Yes, sir!"

Elvis started to turn and leave, but Pickney's words stopped him cold in the back doorway.

"If you fail, kill her, and then do yourself a favor and kill yourself, Elvis. You understand?"

He did not even turn around. He understood completely.

FIFTEEN

Clint was awakened by a soft knocking on his door. When he moved, he groaned, for the pain of his beating hurt worse the second day than it had the first. His cracked ribs radiated pain up through every extremity and his stomach was so tender he could hardly stand to sit up.

"Who is it?"

Juan Escobar began to speak in Spanish with such excitement that it was all a stream of gibberish to the Gunsmith, but he could tell that there was something very wrong.

Clint pushed himself to his feet and grabbed his pants. It took three times as long to pull them on as it would have under ordinary circumstances, but he managed. "I can't understand a single word you're saying, Juan. Where's Mrs. Turner?"

More excited babbling.

Clint grabbed his six-gun and hobbled to the door. He threw it open and listened to the Mexican shepherd for another minute while his head cleared of sleep. Finally, the Gunsmith patted the young Mexican on the shoulder and said, "*Es* okay? Uh?"

"No, no, señor! *Es no* okay! Señora *iba!*"

Clint blinked with astonishment. He shuffled over to the other bedroom and banged on Milly's door. When there was no answer, he pushed the door open and shoved his way into the room. Milly's bed had obviously been slept in, but she was gone.

Clint spun around and hurried out to face Juan. "Where did she go?"

The young shepherd grabbed Clint by the arm and pulled him outside. He pointed toward Pine Bluff and, from the expression on his anxious young face, it was clear that he thought that Milly was as good as dead already.

"Damn!" Clint exclaimed. "Why didn't you wake me up when she left?"

Juan almost looked to be in tears. *"No comprende! No comprende!"*

Clint nodded. "Of course you don't understand. I don't understand you, you don't understand me. But I'll bet anything that Milly told you to let me sleep and not interfere in whatever crazy scheme she had in mind."

Clint rushed back into the house and finished dressing. When he came out again, he discovered that Juan already had saddled a horse. Clint was grateful. Probably because of his beating, he had slept later than usual. By the looks of the sun, it was midmorning. Whatever Milly had in mind, she most likely had done it by now, and Clint had a sick feeling that she was either dead or in serious trouble.

The Gunsmith shook his head and then checked his gun and rifle. He would be riding into bad trouble. Maybe an ambush or a trap. He looked over at the Mexican who stood before a saddled horse. Clint knew that the young man was going to rabbit and run. And why not? Juan wouldn't last five seconds in Pine Bluff before someone gunned him down or beat him so badly he would not return to this ranch ever again.

"Adios, Juan!"

The Mexican looked up. *"Adios, hombre,"* he whispered.

Clint set the horse he rode into a gallop and headed for Pine Bluff. He was not yet sure of how in the world he was going to save Milly—if she was still alive. But if there was any chance at all, he would take it and get her out of trouble. He remembered Dora had said it was Milly who had the brains of the Turner family. Well, this morning proved only one thing—neither of the Turners were very goddam long on good sense. One was dead, and the other would be soon, if she wasn't already.

When he rode into town, Clint had the feeling that dozens of eyes were watching him. He trotted his horse down Main Street and then angled toward the offices of Sierra Timber. Clint supposed there were a lot smarter ways to approach trouble than to do it directly, but he was out of patience and out of time. His lips were crusted with dried blood and his face was swollen from the brass knuckles that had been used on him yesterday by Elvis Tate. When he found that man, he was going to challenge him to a gunfight.

Clint rode up to the hitching post in front of Sierra Timber and dismounted. There were at least six men lounging around in front of the building and when they saw him, they stopped talking and their hands eased toward their guns. The two men that had held his arms yesterday while Elvis Tate had beat him half to death were not in sight nor was Tate himself.

The man who detached himself from the group and stepped forward matched the description that Clint had of Pickney. He was tall, slender, and he looked evil to Clint. His gun was tied down and when he spoke, he had a Texas drawl.

"That's far enough," he said. "In fact, you can get back on your horse and just keep riding the hell out of this part of the country. It's the one and only time I am going to give you that piece of healthy advice."

"I'm looking for Milly Turner."

"Maybe she rode over to California. Why don't you look there?"

Clint shook his head. "I saw her horse tied about a block over. My guess is that she came here."

"You guess wrong."

Clint smiled. He knew there was no way that he could out-draw and kill them all. The odds of surviving a gunfight against so many were zero and none.

"I want to see Jeb Oatman."

Pickney shook his head. "You got one last warning, Gunsmith. Get back on your horse and ride the hell out of Nevada."

"I don't think I'll do that," Clint said. "You got two choices. Get Jeb Oatman out here, or draw. Your choice."

Pickney's eyes flicked to the men surrounding him. "You can't win," he said, looking back at Clint. "If I don't get you, one of these men will."

"So it would appear. Now, make up your mind."

Pickney had not wanted it to work out this way. He was not a fool, nor was he some starry-eyed young reputation-seeker. He was fast, very fast but had never faced a man of the Gunsmith's caliber. He wanted to back down, but with all the men watching, he knew that was impossible. Trapped, he said, "Boys, if I go down, you better finish the job."

Clint studied the gunmen and when he saw the weakest among them, he spoke directly to the man. "Why don't you go ask your boss to come on out and talk? 'Cause if you don't, my second bullet has your name on it."

The gunman shifted on the balls of his feet. "Pickney," he blurted, "what harm could there be by my telling Mr. Oatman that the Gunsmith wants to talk? Huh? What harm?"

"No harm," Jeb Oatman said, pushing the door to his office open. "No harm at all."

He looked right at Clint. "I always thought that for a lawman to survive in the West, he had to have some intelligence. Obviously, that doesn't apply to you."

"Nor to you," Clint said, studying the powerful owner of Sierra Timber. "I guess Mrs. Turner came to see you. Now, the only thing I want to know is if she is dead or alive."

Oatman shrugged. "How should I know? I haven't seen the woman. But I admit that I was planning to ride out and pay my condolences. Who knows, she might even decide that holding onto that ranch isn't such a good idea anymore."

"Where is she?" Clint demanded.

Oatman's voice took on an edge. "I told you, I don't know. Now, I think you and I could do business if we managed to get off on the right foot. Don't you, Pickney?"

Pickney said nothing, but the back of his neck reddened because Jeb Oatman knew that he had not wanted to draw against the Gunsmith. For the first time in his life, Pickney had hesitated and, in his profession, hesitations were almost always fatal.

"Why don't you come inside, Gunsmith? I don't often get to visit with a legend in his own time."

Clint thought about it for a moment. He might be walking into a trap, but on the other hand, he might also learn something that would be of great value. It was Clint's experience that men like Oatman were usually so cocky and overconfident that they often bragged and said more than they should. "All right," he said.

Clint followed Oatman into his plush office. It was decorated with baroque furniture. Heavy, expensive drapes covered the windows and the rugs were deep and ornately woven. The man's desk was huge and there was a silver box filled with cigars sitting beside a gold pen set.

And off to one side stood Sheriff Ford and Deputy Rangles.

"Boys," Oatman said, "I guess you have already had the pleasure of meeting the famous Gunsmith."

Ford actually grinned, but his cocky young deputy looked ready to kill.

Clint did not know what was going to happen, but he decided to play along with the game in hopes that one of them would make a slip. "Sheriff," he said, "Milly Turner rode into town this morning. Her horse is over on Main Street, but she's missing. I think she came here and I think this man has either killed or abducted her."

"She ain't dead!"

Clint turned to the deputy. "Is that a fact? How would you know?"

Rangles blushed with fury, realizing his temper and his mouth had gotten the better of his good sense. Sheriff Ford, however, came to his rescue and proved his sharp intelligence. "Because no one has heard a shot fired in Pine Bluff since around midnight. That's how you know, isn't it Rangles?"

"That's right!" Rangles looked pathetically relieved to be off the hook.

Clint said, "But she might have been stabbed or knocked out and abducted. She might even be lying unconscious in some alley. Sheriff, it's your office's responsibility to begin a search for the young woman."

Oatman agreed. "Sheriff, while I'm sure Mrs. Turner is probably just visiting friends in town to share her grief, we can't be too certain. Why don't you send your deputy along with a couple of my boys and start a search? If Mrs. Turner doesn't show up by noon, come on back."

Ford nodded to his deputy. "You heard Mr. Oatman. Go find the Turner woman and come on back."

Rangles nodded. He was wising up a little and ready to play the game. "Sure, sure I will," he said, refusing to even look at Clint. "Like you say, Mr. Oatman, she's probably visiting friends. If she's hereabouts, we'll find her."

Rangles left them. Oatman took a seat behind his desk and the sheriff eased his massive bulk into a protesting chair. Oatman ignored the fat man and his eyes appraised Clint with a mixture of respect and wary regard. "I've heard stories about you for years, Gunsmith. I heard you've outdrawn every man you ever faced."

"There's no room for being second-best in that profession."

"No, I suppose not," Oatman said. "I don't like men who are second-best. I thought Pickney was the fastest man alive. And maybe he is. But you just backed him down despite the fact that he had a crowd of men standing behind him."

Clint shrugged. "Pickney knew it was him or me either way."

"Would you be willing to become Sheriff Ford's new deputy?" Oatman asked.

Clint was surprised by the blunt offer. "What about Rangles?"

"He just proved to me he doesn't think before he speaks," Oatman said. "That can get a man into big trouble in a hurry. I think you ought to discharge him and hire Mr. Adams. Don't you, Sheriff?"

Ford nodded but he looked mighty worried. "I don't think the Gunsmith will take the job," he managed to say.

Oatman looked at Clint. "Your deputy's pay would be three hundred a month, and there are some side benefits we can talk about later. Also, Sheriff Ford has been thinking about retirement, and you could find yourself being promoted real soon with a nice raise. How about it, Gunsmith?"

Clint looked at the sheriff, whose mouth was hanging open. He wanted to say yes just to see if Ford would even dare to lodge a protest. But instead, Clint shook his head. "Not interested."

Oatman frowned. "What a pity. Sheriff, I think you had better step outside and tell Mr. Pickney that he and the boys be ready to accept Mr. Adams' earlier offer to fight. It would seem that the Gunsmith is tired of living."

The sheriff got up and he was pale. He went to the door and just before his hand touched the handle, Clint was on his feet and his gun was in his fist. "If you open that door, you'll never walk through it alive."

Sheriff Ford's hand hung motionless in the air. "I . . . I just want to resign my office," he stammered. "I don't want to die."

Clint went over to the man and removed the gun from his holster. "Now, move over by the wall and don't say a word."

Clint turned back to face Oatman. The man was standing up now and his face was composed. He said, "If you kill me, you'll never have a chance to get out of here alive and the girl will die."

"I thought you didn't know where she was," Clint said.

"I don't. It doesn't matter if you believe me or not about that part of it. But if I die, so will she."

Clint knew he was facing a stand-off. Oatman was clever. He had insured his life with that of Milly Turner.

"Sheriff," Clint said, reaching a quick decision, "you and I are getting out of here. If you haven't figured it out yet, your days are numbered in Pine Bluff. Help me get to my horse and I'll let you ride out of town."

Ford nodded so vigorously his jowls shook. "All I ask is that we stop by the bank on the way out. I got savings there. I'm too damn old and fat to start over with nothing."

"It's a deal," Clint said, putting his gun into his holster. He stepped over to the desk and, without warning, he doubled up his fist and drove it into Oatman's hooked nose. The nose broke and bled and Oatman grabbed his face and staggered backward.

"That's for what your men did to me yesterday," Clint said.

Oatman looked up and his black eyes were murderous. "You won't live to see sundown," he said in a thick voice.

"Don't bet on it." Clint shoved Ford toward the door. "Come on," he said, "let's get out of here."

The sheriff was as ready to leave Pine Bluff as the Gunsmith.

SIXTEEN

Clint stood outside the door of the bank and waited for Doug Ford to come out with his money. He hadn't wanted to help Ford at all, but if he could get the ex-sheriff out of Pine Bluff, then he'd demand to know where Oatman had hidden Milly Turner. It seemed like a fair enough swap for the Gunsmith, and it might be his only chance to save Milly.

It took Ford less than five minutes to hurry outside with a sack of money. Clint stared at it and said, "I can see that he must have paid you well. It galls the hell out of me to be forced to help you get out of this town alive."

Ford grinned. Now that he had his money in hand, he seemed almost jubilant. "Mister, I think I owe you a hell of a lot. Sooner or later, that murdering deputy was going to grow tired of waiting for his time to be sheriff. I figured I had less than three more months before either Rangles or Oatman himself decided I was through. Let's get the hell out of here."

"How?" Clint asked, knowing that no ordinary horse could carry the ex-sheriff.

"I always travel in a buggy," the man said. "It's mine and I got a fine sorrel mare that can pull it as pretty as you please. She and the buggy both are out behind my office. Let's get the hell out of this town."

Clint agreed. He followed the huge sheriff across the street and down the alley until they came to a corral. The buggy was humble, but Clint figured it would carry the sheriff's weight at least as far as Mormon Station, and the man could walk the rest of the way to Carson City and safety if necessary.

Ford could move faster than you'd think for a truly obese man. Though the temperature was only in the mid-seventies, he was sweating heavily as he hauled the harness out of his office and quickly hitched up the buggy to the sorrel mare.

"I'll ride with you to the city limits and then you're on your own," the Gunsmith said, hefting his Winchester and keeping his eye out for approaching trouble.

"That's plenty far enough." Ford hauled his great bulk into the wagon and the braces sagged. "Oatman knows I'm not going to say a damn thing to you."

"Are you sure it'll stand the weight of us both?" Clint asked, deciding that this was not the time or the place to tell the ex-sheriff that he had damn sure better tell him about Milly Turner.

"Hell, yes," Ford said. "Get in!"

Clint jumped in and the buggy almost broke in the middle. Ford applied the whip smartly, and the sorrel threw her shoulders into the harness and the buggy rolled forward. Ford slapped her again with the whip, and the buggy picked up speed as it rolled down the back streets heading north. They passed through the residential part of town, and Clint breathed a sigh of relief when they left everything behind and were in open country.

A mile out, the sheriff pulled the sorrel to a halt. "I guess this is far enough, Gunsmith. I don't imagine you enjoy walking anymore than the next fella. I thank you for delivering me from that place. I've been a walking dead man for over a year. It was just a matter of when they planted me."

Clint unholstered his gun and pointed it at the fat man. "It isn't that easy, Ford. I have to know what they did with Milly Turner."

The sheriff shook his head. "If I told you what I know, I'd be among the walking dead again."

"You don't seem to understand," Clint said patiently. "If

you don't tell me right now, you're going to the promised land right now."

But Ford shook his head. "Uh-uh. You won't shoot me. It's against your own code. I know something about human nature. I've studied men—good and bad ones—all my life, and I'm an excellent judge of character. Probably because I don't have much character of my own. But the thing that matters is that I knew from the start that you'd never accept Oatman's offer. But he wouldn't listen. The bastard believes every man ever born has a price tag. I had mine and so does Rangles. You don't. I guess I didn't hardly believe it myself until I met you. An honest lawman is a rare thing."

Clint cocked the gun and shoved it into the man's blubbery side. "I don't want no high-sounding lectures on human nature, dammit! Tell me about Milly Turner."

"I can't," the man said. "She's as good as dead already. And you aren't going to pull the trigger of that gun so why don't we just shake hands and part as friends?"

Clint stepped down from the buggy. "You were a crooked sheriff, and that means you'd be no friend of mine. Get the hell out of my sight."

Ford nodded sadly. "I don't blame you. You want my advice, you get out of town and forget all about Milly Turner."

Ford started to lift the whip, but Clint grabbed his reins. "How can you drive away and let that woman be murdered? Can you really live with yourself?"

"Yep," Ford said, "I sure as hell can."

Clint was afraid he was going to lose control of his temper and shoot the fat man dead if he didn't let him get out of his sight. "Get the hell out of here!" the Gunsmith hissed, releasing the reins. "You make me sick!"

Ford lashed the mare and the buggy took off fast. Clint stood and watched it, feeling nothing but a powerful sense of defeat. Ford had been too damn smart for him. The man had known right from the start that Clint would not shoot him in cold blood. The Gunsmith turned his back and headed toward town. He wasn't sure what he was going to do next. All he knew was that he hadn't a single clue as to Milly's whereabouts.

A booming rifleshot cut across the sage-covered land. Clint whirled and a second shot followed. Clint saw the buggy, now almost a half mile away, veer sharply, and then he saw Ford tumble out of his seat and crash to the earth. The buggy raced on. Ford tried to crawl toward a gully. The large-caliber hunting rifle boomed again, and Ford sagged to the earth and lay still.

Clint started running toward the man. The rifle opened up on him, and the Gunsmith began to run a crooked pattern in a desperate attempt to reach the ex-sheriff. A bullet clipped off one of his heels and the Gunsmith went sprawling to the ground as more bullets bit into the earth all around him. Clint got up and started running again. His broken ribs slowed him down, but he still managed to reach a patch of heavy sagebrush and dive for cover.

The ambushers began to shoot into the brush, spacing their bullets in a pattern designed to maximize their chances of a kill. They were experts, every damned one of them. Clint inched forward and when he could see where the shots were coming from, he poked his own rifle out in front of him and pressed his cheek to the walnut stock of his gun and squeezed down on the trigger. When a puff of smoke blossomed from a stand of distant trees, Clint aimed high and fired.

A man staggered into plain view and then crashed to the ground. He began to howl and scream. One of the bushwackers made the fatal mistake of trying to reach his friend, and Clint's next shot knocked him over like a bowling pin. He rolled once and lay still.

Clint moved quickly to one side, and it was well that he did for an angry swarm of lead cut into the brush where he had lain. The Gunsmith fired three more quick shots and then moved again. If the bastards were going to kill him, he figured he'd disrupt their target pattern so badly that they would be forced to drive him out of his cover. Clint didn't think they'd want to do that.

He was right. The ambushers continued shooting, but now their efforts were hurried and disorganized. After an hour and one more of their number being wounded, they vanished into the trees. Five minutes later, Clint saw the dust from their horses on the far horizon. He stood up, rifle to his chest and ready. Nothing moved and when he was sure that it was safe to proceed, the Gunsmith went to inspect the body of Doug Ford.

The ex-sheriff of Pine Bluff was not quite ready to die. He had three rifle bullets in his bloated body and he had lost a great deal of blood, but his heart still beat and his eyes were open when Clint reached his side. He was breathing rapidly and his face was chalky white.

"Are they all dead?" he rattled

"No," Clint said, easing himself down beside the dying man. "I just run them off."

Ford licked his lips and tried to swallow. "I can't see but it doesn't hurt. I guess I'm finished."

One of the bullet holes was through a lung, and Clint knew there was no sense in lying to the man. There wasn't a thing in the world anyone could do for Doug Ford anymore. "Yeah, you're finished. You want to tell me where Milly Turner was taken this morning?"

"All right," the man wheezed. "I wouldn't have if they'd have let me go. I wouldn't have betrayed Oatman, only he's the one who ordered this done."

The dying man began to cough violently. Bright red bubbles covered his lips. Clint was afraid he was going to expire before he had a chance to say another word. The Gunsmith gripped the man's thick arm and said, "Who took Milly and where is she?"

"Elvis Tate and the two men who helped him beat you have got her in the mountains."

"Where?"

Ford's great body convulsed, and his eyes widened as a great seizure shook him. His mouth worked in silence and just before he stiffened and died, he whispered, "I . . . don't know. Somewhere in. . . ."

Clint shook him. "Tell me!"

"Mountains!" Ford gasped. "Cabin in mountains!"

He grabbed Clint's shirtfront and then he was gone.

Clint stood and looked up at the great range of Sierra Nevada Mountains. They stretched for hundreds of miles north and south from the Oregon Territory as far south as Death Valley. The Gunsmith had no illusions that Jeb Oatman would be stupid enough to have Milly taken to a cabin somewhere close by. In fact, Clint decided that it would be a complete waste of time to even look to the mountains that towered above this particular valley.

But he had to have some idea where to start. Clint took a deep breath and figured he'd just have to do what he'd always done when he was fresh out of clues—he'd talk to people. A lot of people. Someone must have seen Milly Turner being taken out of town—unless she was thrown into the bed of a freight wagon and covered with a tarp or something.

Clint didn't even want to consider that possibility.

SEVENTEEN

Milly Turner felt the wagon bounce and jolt along the dirt road. She was almost suffocating from the heavy canvas tarpaulin that covered her and the gag in her mouth. Bound hand and foot, Milly felt as trussed-up as an ewe being hauled off to slaughter. And that was not a bad analogy given the terrible fix she had gotten herself into.

It made her furious that she might die before she even had a chance to avenge her late husband's death. She now realized that she had been a fool to suppose that she might brazenly waltz into Oatman's almost fortified offices, just happen to find him and Elvis Tate conveniently sitting together, then shoot them both before anyone could stop her.

Hell, Milly thought, I didn't even get to his front door!

She struggled mightily against the ropes that bound her but they were so tight that her hands and feet were numb, and there was no way to move around in the wagon without alerting the men up front in the wagon seat. So all she could do was to wait and see what they would do with her once they reached their destination. Milly realized that she had been unconscious and therefore had completely lost track of time. Because she was blindfolded and shrouded in darkness, it could be day or night.

She dozed on and off and realized that the wagon had begun to climb into the mountains. In waking moments, she could hear the men talking and knew that one of them was Elvis Tate. And though it seemed preposterous, she still

105

maintained the hope that she might somehow get a gun and shoot the man who had murdered her husband.

Where were they taking her and for what purpose? Milly was almost afraid to even consider those two questions. At any minute she expected the wagon to grind to a stop, and the men would pull her out, shoot her to death, and then throw her down some isolated canyon where she would be carrion for wild animals. Equally terrible was the thought that she might be taken to some cabin and tortured while being held hostage for the title of her ranch. This latter possibility seemed more likely with each hour that passed.

Milly grew cold and figured it was nighttime and that they were high in the Sierras. She could smell the pine trees all around her and hear the sound of a river as it tumbled down a steep canyon. Her anxiety increased by the hour, and when the wagon finally came to a halt and she felt the weight of men tip the wagon three times, she knew that they had reached their destination.

Cold terror filled her heart. She struggled like a rabbit caught by the neck in a noose, and it did no good. Tears stung her eyes and she railed at her own weakness and fear. Her throat was so dry that it felt as if she were swallowing sand. She had to urinate and she felt humiliated by the situation she was now forced to endure.

They left her in the wagon for a long time while they unloaded the wagon, unhitched the team, and built a fire. They talked little among themselves, and when Milly finally smelled bacon and beans, her empty stomach churned. She was amazed that food still appealed to her senses, given her pathetic circumstances.

"All right," Elvis Tate called, as he pulled the tarpaulin back and grabbed her by the ankles. "The ride is over."

Milly kicked blindly at his face, but he yanked her out of the wagon, grabbed her like a sack of oats, and threw her over his shoulder to carry her up a steep path. When he stepped through a doorway, he dumped her on the dirt floor, and Milly heard them all laughing.

"Take her blindfold off and get the gag out of her mouth," Elvis said.

"You sure you want to do that?" another man asked. "Right now, she's quiet and we can pretty much do what we want with her."

To her horror, Milly felt a man's hand on her leg. She tried to scream but the gag choked her.

"Get away from her!" Elvis shouted. "I told you, if she cooperates, we let her go."

Milly did not believe a word of it. Elvis' words had the ring of a well-rehearsed little speech, and she knew damn well that these men could not afford to let her go.

The blindfold was taken from her face and she looked at the three leering gunmen. When Elvis bent over and tore the gag out of her mouth, she tried to spit on him but her mouth was as dry as the desert.

"You're a real little hellcat, ain't you," Elvis said, with a trace of admiration in his voice. "It's a damn shame you ain't got brains to match your guts."

Milly had a reply, but her throat was in such bad shape that when she spoke, the words came out nothing but a whisper. The three men thought this was very funny and laughed. Elvis took out a pocket knife and cut her bonds and said, "Set the damn table and be quick about it."

"Go to hell!" she muttered.

The gunman's hand darted out and when his fist struck Milly, she went sprawling. "I won't help you animals," she panted, trying to push herself erect. She was determined to show no fear.

Elvis walked over to stand above her. "Well, boys," he said, "then I guess we're going to have to teach her how to start pleasing real men."

To Milly's horror, Elvis Tate began to unbutton his pants. "Wait!" she heard herself cry. "All right! I'll cook and clean if you'll just leave me alone."

Elvis reluctantly rebuttoned his pants. "Have it your own way," he said. "But you better cooperate with us or we're going to have our fun."

Milly tried to keep her lip from trembling. She was ashamed as her courage just seemed to shrivel up and die. This . . . this animal had beaten her so damned easily. Just as easily as he had killed poor, brave Abner.

Milly could not help herself—she began to cry.

EIGHTEEN

The Gunsmith rode toward the Turner ranch grim-faced and resolute in his determination to find Milly Turner within the next few days. She was his number-one priority but after her, there was a long list of debts owed, starting with Elvis Tate and the high and mighty Mr. Oatman himself. Clint knew full well that he would also have to take on a small army of gunmen.

As he approached the Turner ranch, the Gunsmith reined his horse in and dismounted. He stepped behind the animal and drew his rifle, because a highly refined warning system was telling him that someone was waiting for him.

Clint looped his reins over the horse's neck and set the animal free. The horse moved toward the barn, and Clint followed it closely, exposing himself to a waiting rifleman as little as possible. Clint had already been nearly killed enough times in one day, and a man could push his luck too far.

A strong wind blew off the mountains and the barn door was banging against the doorframe. Clint waited until the last possible moment and then he sprinted toward the bunkhouse and went crashing inside.

"Juan?"

There was no answer in the dim interior of the room. Juan Escobar's bedroll and things were gone and the only thing left belonging to the brothers was a crude wooden crucifix. Clint picked himself up off the floor with the rifle still clenched in his hands, but it occurred to him that maybe he was starting to get spooked and imagine things. The ranch was deserted.

Clint went back outside and crouched in the open doorway. Something was very wrong. And then it struck him what was missing—the sheepdogs. There was not a sign of them anywhere. But maybe they were all out with the flock.

He decided to check out the ranch house to make sure it was empty. Starting across the yard, he suddenly had a feeling of great danger. It was crazy, but his instincts had saved his life many times in his career and the Gunsmith was not about to ignore the warning signals now. Despite his ribs, he dropped to the dirt and rolled, bringing the rifle up.

It was well that he did, for Deputy Rangles jumped out into the yard and pumped two fast shots at the Gunsmith. When Clint fired, his shot sent the deputy diving for cover. Clint got up and dashed for his own cover.

"Rangles!"

"Yeah," the young deputy called.

"I misjudged you for a man who stood up and fought face to face. Are you a cowardly back-shooter?" Clint shouted.

Rangles stepped out from cover and holstered his gun. He spread his legs apart and said, "Let's see who really is the fastest man."

Clint thought about it for a moment. He had two choices, he could draw against the younger man and there was a chance he could lose. If that happened, not only would he forfeit his own life, but Milly Turner's as well. The second choice he had was to just ventilate this young fool with his Winchester and be done with Rangles once and for all.

The choice was surprisingly easy. Clint raised the rifle to his shoulder, took aim and sent a bullet through Rangle's right forearm. The deputy screamed in pain and tried to draw his six-gun but his bones and tendons were mangled.

"You dirty sonofabitch!" he screamed in rage. "You tricked me!"

Clint stood up and shrugged his shoulders. "I never made you any promises, did I?"

Clint walked quickly across the yard as Rangles fumbled to reach his gun with his left hand. The deputy did manage to draw his weapon, but he dropped it in the dirt.

"Leave it alone and ride out of this valley while you're still alive," the Gunsmith warned.

The deputy hesitated. He wanted to pick his gun up so bad that he fairly trembled. But fear and caution penetrated his mind. Rangles was not a fool and he must have understood that against the Gunsmith and with his left hand, he would have no chance at all. "I could have beaten you!"

"Maybe, but I outsmarted you and sometimes, that's worth a lot more than speed with a six-gun. You're stupid and corrupt, Rangles. You wanted to kill me in hopes that Oatman would decide you were man enough to be the next sheriff. But you aren't and you never will be. Find honest work and try and turn your life around before it's too late."

"Go to hell!"

Clint bent down and grabbed the man by his lapels and dragged him to his feet. This kid was a snake and did not even have the shred of honor that Doug Ford had possessed. "I want to know where they took Milly Turner."

"How should I know! Even Oatman himself doesn't know."

"You can give me some idea," Clint said through clenched teeth. "You must have seen them leave. Was it in a freight wagon, or what?"

Rangles was in agony. "I'm bleeding to death!" he cried. "I need a doctor."

"Better a doctor than a mortician. That's what you'll get if you don't start giving me some answers."

"All right. Tate and two others took her to a cabin somewhere in the Sierras."

"That's not good enough!"

"It's all I know! I swear it is!"

Clint looked into the deputy's eyes. The man was terrified. He didn't figure to be lying. "Where's your horse?"

Hope sprang into the deputy's eyes. "You gonna let me go?"

"I guess."

Rangles stared at him. "You and Dora . . . she likes you."

"We go back a ways," Clint said. "You leave her the hell alone or I'll put the next bullet right where your legs meet and you'll never have another woman as long as you live."

"Oatman and his men will kill you for sure."

"He'll try." Clint studied the man, whose eyes were ringed with pain. "Maybe you ought to know that some of his boys ambushed me and Ford about two miles north of Pine Bluff. They killed the sheriff. Shot him three times, once right through the lungs. Seems to me that the day would have come when they'd have ordered your death, too."

Rangles blinked. "They ambushed old Doug Ford. Why, he wouldn't have said nothing against Oatman!"

"I know, but they figured he might. Either way, he's dead and you have every right to be. I'm giving you a second chance to start over again. That's better than you'd ever have gotten from the men who paid you to clear out their opposition."

Rangles untied the bandanna from around his neck. "You want to give me a hand?"

Clint took the bandanna and tied it over the bullet wound. That finished, he turned and headed for the barn. He was going to try and put a new horseshoe on Duke and see if the big gelding was fit enough for the trail.

"Gunsmith!"

Clint threw himself to the earth as he drew his six-gun. He twisted and the weapon in his fist bucked twice, and Rangles, his own gun jerking in his left hand, emptied three bullets into the dirt.

"Once a man loses all honor, he almost never gets it back," Clint said. Then he turned and headed for the barn.

•   •   •

Abner Turner had a good toolshed, anvil, and forge, and though Clint was not an accomplished blacksmith, he was like many long riders in that he knew how to shape a shoe that had already been made. And there were plenty of those around the shop, some worn almost completely through at the toes, others looking to be in good shape. Clint tried a few of the good ones on Duke and when he found a shoe that came close to making a fit, he tacked it on and set the gelding's foot down.

Finding his bridle, he led the big gelding out of his stall and then walked him around the barn. Satisfied that Duke's rock bruise had healed enough so that the horse was no longer in pain, Clint saddled him quickly.

"We got a lot of mountain to search," he told the horse. "It's going to be tough going, but Milly Turner's life is at stake. I need you under me if I got any chance at all."

The gelding seemed to understand and nodded his fine head. And when Clint put a foot in the stirrup and climbed stiffly into the saddle, even his ribs felt better for riding on his big gelding.

He reined the horse out of the barn and headed north without so much as a backward glance at Rangles, who was lying sprawled in the ranch yard.

It had sure been one hell of a bloody day.

NINETEEN

Clint rode about five miles south until he came to the Turner flock of sheep. He had expected to see them scattered all over the mountainside but instead, they were nicely banded together. Juan Escobar waved to him in greeting and the four sheepdogs he had with him barked with excitement.

"What about Mexico?" Clint said, pointing at the shepherd and then twisting around in his saddle and pointing south. "Juan go to Mexico?"

The shepherd shook his head. He pointed at his dogs. "Dogs no go, Juan no go Mexico, either. Sheep need."

Clint smiled, for he had always suspected the Mexican could speak broken English if it suited his purpose. "Well, I'll be darned. So your conscience got the better of you, did it?"

"No comprende, señor."

"Oh, I'll be bet you *comprende* plenty. Well, I better get moving. *Adios,* señor!"

Clint started to leave but Jaun stepped in his way. "Señor...uh, Señora Turner?"

Clint raised his hands palm up in a clear gesture that left no doubt that he did not know where the woman had been taken. He then pointed up at the Sierras and said, "Señora Turner up there."

Juan understood. He turned and looked at his flock and called to his dogs. He spoke to them rapidly in his native tongue and when he finished, he sent all but one of them out to watch the flock while he went to his horse and began to saddle up.

"Hey!" Clint said. "What are you up to?"

Juan smiled. "Help Señora Turner."

"Can you shoot straight?"

Juan shrugged. Clint took out his rifle and dismounted. He saw a pinecone about fifty paces ahead, and he threw the rifle to his shoulder and blew it to smithereens. Then he handed the rifle to the shepherd and motioned for him to do the same.

Juan's face lit up and he caressed the Winchester for a moment, admiring its quality. Then he pointed to a little rock about the size of Clint's fist. It lay at a distance of about sixty yards, and the Mexican laid his cheek on the stock, squinted, and fired. He missed by at least ten feet.

Handing the rifle back to Clint, he grinned and shrugged as if to say that he was very sorry.

"I think you'd be better to stay with the flock, Juan," Clint said as he shoved the rifle back into its scabbard and remounted. Clint touched spurs and rode away. But fifteen minutes later, the Mexican was galloping up behind him, his face very serious. He had an old flintlock rifle that he probably used to scare the coyotes away from his flock of sheep. The weapon looked as if its barrel had been used as a pry bar. It didn't appear to have ever been cleaned and the front sight was banged down flat. One glance at the rifle told Clint everything. Juan had never needed to kill, with a rifle such as he used, you scare anything that moved—including a professional gunman.

The Mexican had filled a huge, multicolored serape with food and tied it behind his cantle. He was wearing a sombrero and there was an old cap-and-ball, .36 caliber Navy Colt pistol stuck in a red sash wrapped around his waist. Clint almost smiled because the man looked more like a swashbuckling pirate than a poor Mexican shepherd.

"Juan," he said, "I really think you ought to turn back. You can't shoot and those weapons of yours scare the hell outa me."

"Si, Señor Cleent!" Juan reached around behind him and rummaged in his pack. He selected a handful of tortillas and offered them to Clint, who took two and then watched the shepherd eat the rest with gusto. Actually, the tortillas were good and Clint had not eaten in a long while. "Got any more in there?"

"Si!"

Clint chuckled as he took some more. "Don't try to play dumb with me, Juan. I just proved you could speak English."

Chomping on a mouthful of tortillas, Juan shrugged and mumbled something that Clint could not understand but which sounded like, *"No comprende."*

Three days later, Clint had a break. He had been riding from mountain pass to mountain pass and all the cabins he could see in between asking if anyone had seen a wagon being driven by a red-haired man and two sidekicks. Elvis Tate, with his bright red hair, was a man whose appearance attracted attention.

"Yeah, I saw him," a driver growled as he looked down at Clint and the shepherd from his lofty position high up on the seat of a big freight wagon. "It was on my last trip over Carson Pass. They was coming up the mountain and I was going down. I remember that redheaded sonofabitch didn't want to give me enough room. There was a steep drop on my side, and I guess he didn't give a damn if I went over or not. I gave him and his team a taste of my blacksnake and my mind."

"Where was it, exactly?"

The freighter told him. Then came the real surprise as the man added, "I can tell you something else you'll like hearing even better. Them three jaspers cut off the main road on a logging trail going north. It leads up about five miles and then dead-ends. Used to be a lot of timber cut up there, but it's pretty well logged off now. Cabin sits all alone out in the open."

Clint curbed his own rising sense of excitement. "You're sitting pretty high up there. Could you see down in the wagon?"

"They weren't hauling any freight. The team they was driving wasn't hardly sweatin' any. Just some covered-up stuff is all."

"Mister, you don't know how much help you've been," Clint said. "I can't thank you enough."

"Just beat the hell outa that red-haired sonofabitch if you find him. I know, if I find him, that's what I'll do."

Clint did not bother to warn the freighter that Elvis Tate was a professional gunman who would shoot him dead in his tracks at the slightest provocation.

There was no need to give a warning. The freighter would never see Tate alive again.

Juan checked his rifle and nodded with satisfaction. His young face showed that he was full of anxiety but committed to seeing this thing through to the very end.

"I still wish you'd have stayed with your flock," Clint said to the Mexican. "I don't want to be anywhere close when you pull the trigger on either one of those cannons."

Juan shrugged and, perfectly straight-faced, said, "A man does the best he can, eh, Señor Gunsmith?"

Clint blinked with amazement. "Juan, you're worth a-plenty, all right. And in truth, I'm glad to have your company. But when it comes down to fighting, I expect you to take my orders. Savvy?"

"Sure." The shepherd nodded. "I do this not only for the Señor, but for my brother and the honor of my family. Comprende?"

"You bet," Clint said. "Let's go get them!"

TWENTY

The freighter had known what he was talking about. Clint and Juan followed the logging road for about six miles, and then suddenly they came upon an entire mountainside that had been stripped clean of all timber. The sight of thousands of stumps and acre upon acre of dead limbs that had been trimmed away from the trunks of their trees left a deep impression on the Gunsmith.

Even the Mexican, accustomed to the open country of Northern Mexico, was shocked, and whispered, *"Por dios!"*

"Yes," Clint said, staring at the devestation. "My thoughts exactly."

He dismounted and Juan followed suit. The Gunsmith wondered why the loggers had suddenly stopped their destruction, until he began to study the pines around him. They were much smaller in diameter than the stump field that lay between him and the cabin several miles ahead. For some reason, soil, sunlight, perhaps, these pines just had not grown as tall or as thick and therefore were not as profitable for logging companies.

"I never saw anything that looked so bad as this," Clint said, tying Duke up where he could not be seen. "We'll have a hell of a time just climbing through all that deadfall getting to the cabin. Sure can't go up the road."

Juan nodded. His dog, a big male with a brown-and-white coat, whined softly.

Clint knelt to pat the animal's head. A low rumble in the

119

dog's throat and his bared teeth convinced Clint that the
animal did not want to be petted by anyone except his
master. Clint looked up at the Mexican. "Now I know why
you chose this one. He's the meanest and best fighter of
the lot, isn't that right?"

"Si."

Clint stood up. "I want you to tie him up and keep him
close to you. We can't have him bark, and if he should
decide to run out from cover, those fellas in there might
recognize him as a sheepdog. They'd most likely put two
and two together and come up with four. In that case, they'd
realize that trouble is on its way."

But Juan shook his head. "Sheepdog no tie."

"Tie him, dammit! Our lives and that of Mrs. Turner
could depend upon it."

Juan nodded with great reluctance. He cut the reins from
the bit and fashioned a leash. But when he tied it around
the sheepdog's neck, the animal about went berserk. He
started to jump and fight the leash. Juan tried to control
him, but the noose tightened around the dog's throat and
he began to choke. The Mexican could not stand it and used
his knife to cut the leash away.

"No, señor!"

Clint was not pleased. He hadn't wanted the Mexican
along because he and his damned dog were going to be
more trouble than they were worth. And if the dog started
barking or raising hell, all of their lives would be jeopar-
dized.

"All right, then, you and the dog stay here with the horses
and wait. I'm going to sneak to the cabin and wait until
nightfall, when I'll go in after Milly. Do you understand?"

Juan nodded. "What can I do?"

"Just watch the horses and keep your powder dry," Clint
said. "And I guess, if you hear shooting, come running up
the road because you'd never get through all that deadfall
in the darkness."

"And the dog, señor?"

"Hell, I don't know why you brought him in the first place."

The Mexican looked as if his feelings had been wounded, but Clint did not care. His primary concern was getting Milly out of that cabin alive, and all the good intentions in the world by the shepherd would not advance that goal by one honest inch.

The Gunsmith removed his hat and headed into the dead timber that littered the mountainside, often five and ten feet deep. The dried pine needles crunched under his feet, and when they brushed his hands and face, their sharp points stung his flesh. He had gone less than a hundred yards when he almost stepped on a big timber rattlesnake. The viper rattled its deadly warning, and the Gunsmith tripped over himself in his great haste to get out of its path. Clint swore in frustration. He kept getting tangled up in the dead branches. When he came upon two more rattlesnakes and one struck but glanced off the thick leather of his boots, he was about ready to abandoned this tactic and risk taking the road.

But he kept moving, head down, body in a crouch that soon made his ribs start to ache again and his legs tremble with fatigue. The distance from Juan and the horses to the cabin was about two miles, but it seemed like two hundred to Clint before he finally neared the cabin at sunset.

Making certain that there were no rattlers close by, he slumped to the earth behind a pile of dead limbs, knowing that he could not be seen from the cabin. Clint looked back at the ringed forest of green trees. He figured that, left to his own greed, man could sure mess up God's work in a hurry.

A hawk sailed overhead and just at twilight, one of the gunmen stepped outside and studied the Carson Valley far below. He rolled a cigarette, and Clint watched his face illuminated by the match. The Gunsmith recognized the man as one of the two who had held his arms while Tate used those damn brass knuckles. Clint itched to step out and say something like, "Nice evening, huh, fella?" Then, when the man clawed for his gun, shoot him where he stood.

"Dinner is ready!"

Clint stiffened. It had been Milly Turner's voice he'd heard. A flood of relief filled the Gunsmith as darkness fell across the ugly patch of mountainside. She was alive and well, but Clint knew that made his task far more difficult. Had he merely been intent on capturing or killing these three, it would not have taken too much skill. But to go in there and get Milly away safely, now that was going to take some doing.

Clint knew he was going to need a little luck to pull this off successfully. The problem was, luck ran both hot and cold.

It was almost midnight when the Gunsmith decided that the three men inside the cabin were asleep and it was time to go for Milly. He stood up and walked toward the cabin, gun still in its holster, Winchester resting easy in his hand. It had been more than two hours since the last candle or lamp had been extinguished.

The cabin was small and when Clint reached the door, he could hear snoring inside. He leaned against the wall and considered his next move. The last thing he wanted to do was to start a gunfight in the dark interior of the cabin. With bullets flying in all directions, Milly could be killed by accident, and it would be impossible to get her out to safety.

There is nothing to do but to go inside, light a match, and hope no one wakes up when I go for her, Clint thought. I have to be able to see her in order to get her out fast.

Clint reached into his shirt pocket and found a match. He eased the door open enough to squeeze through and then he scratched the match on the rough wood of the doorframe.

The match flared and illuminated the room brightly for the briefest instant, then the flame drew back and did little more than nudge the corners of the darkness.

The Gunsmith saw four sleeping forms in the room, but

he could not see clearly enough to distinguish which might be the woman. He stepped into the cabin and raised the match overhead. "Milly?" he whispered ever so softly. "It's Clint Adams."

Clint blew out the dying match in his hand and reached for another for he was still not sure which of the figures was Milly Turner. He struck another match and now he finally recognized her. But she was as far from the door as she could be, and he saw that one of her wrists was tied to the stove. Clint frowned and carefully made his way to her side. He blew out the match, then placed his hand over her mouth.

"Milly, wake up!" he whispered.

She stiffened into wakefulness and cried out involuntarily as she tried to lash out with her fingernails to his eyes. Clint had not been expecting such a sudden and violent reaction and was caught by surprise. One of Milly's sharp fingernails ripped the flesh of his cheek. She bit his hand and when he dug his fingers into her cheeks, he was angry. "I said it's me, Clint!"

Milly reached up and examined his face with her fingers in the absolute darkness. "Thank God!" she whispered, apparently satisfied. "Get me out of here."

Clint nodded. It was totally dark in the cabin so he knew that he would have to cut the rope that bound Milly to the stove. To try and untie the damn thing by feel would take forever. "Just hold still," he whispered. "In just a second, I'll have you free and—"

A gunshot roared, and Clint felt something like fire that branded the back of his shoulder. He had been grazed, and the bullet caught enough of his muscle to throw him off balance. He toppled into the stove, and its burnt-out chimney pipe detached from the stove itself and came crashing down into the room. Rust, dust, and ashes billowed up in Clint's face and blinded him. He cursed, choked, and blindly reeled around, hearing Milly's cries of warning.

Someone lit a lamp, and Clint discovered to his great

regret that he was temporarily blinded. Even so, he drew his gun and opened fire. A man screamed, but someone kicked Clint and sent him tumbling over backward. Before Clint could roll to his knees, a gunbarrel was shoved against his skull and the now-familiar voice of Elvis Tate said, "Freeze or die right now!"

Clint froze. His eyes were packed with soot and ash, and they were watering so badly he could scarcely see anything. He knew he had knocked one man out for a good long sleep and that another man had been wounded. But Elvis Tate, it seemed, led a charmed life and had gotten another break.

"Drop your gun and stretch all the way out, facedown on the floor!"

Clint did as he was told. He knew that he could not expect Milly to help because she was still roped to the damned stove. And as for Juan Escobar, what could the Mexican shepherd do?

"Now," Tate said, "you just lie still and don't even think about moving while I see what I can do for—"

Whatever Elvis Tate was going to do was forgotten when Clint heard a low growl as Juan's sheepdog came flying through the door. Tate fired twice. The dog yelped and the terrible rumble in its throat fell silent.

The entire distraction could not have lasted a moment, but it was all the time the Gunsmith needed. His eyes were still filled with tears, but his fingers located his six-gun and he snatched it off the floor and emptied it almost point-blank into Elvis Tate's body.

Juan rushed into the cabin. He took one look around the cabin and saw a wounded gunfighter trying to raise his weapon. Juan closed his eyes, pointed his old Navy Colt at the man and pulled the trigger. The gun actually fired and Clint, through watery eyes, saw the wounded gunfighter crumple.

Juan looked shaken, but he squared his thin shoulders and said, "*Buenas tardes, Señora Turner.*"

To Milly's credit, there was barely the hint of a tremor in

her throat when she replied, "Good evening to you as well, Juan. I thought you were going to Mexico."

"*Mañana*, señora."

"Good," Milly said. "How about cutting me free so I can help our poor but very gallant friend, the Gunsmith?"

"Si." Juan carelessly dropped his old gun on the floor and pulled out a long knife, which he used to quickly cut through Milly's bonds.

"I'm sorry about the dog," she told him. "He was very brave, wasn't he?"

Juan nodded. He scooped up the dog and carried it outside, and while Milly got some water to cleanse out the Gunsmith's eyes, he buried the animal.

"It's just a flesh wound," she told Clint.

"One more to add to the collection," he said drily, thinking how lucky he was and how much he had underestimated Juan and the dog. "The good part is that we got you out of this alive."

"And what's the bad part?"

"We don't have any real proof that Jeb Oatman was behind this. We've killed all the witnesses."

"But he is!" she protested.

"Of course he is," Clint said. "But we have to prove it to a jury. And so far, we're still coming up short."

Milly stared at him and when she spoke, her voice sounded small and defeated. "Just get me out of this place," she said. "Just take me back to the ranch, and I'll be able to face tomorrow."

Clint nodded. His back burned and his ribs were still hurting, but he pushed the pain out of his mind and helped the young widow to her feet and led her outside. At the doorway, he looked back inside and shook his head at the carnage. For a little while, it had seemed as if all the luck was in Elvis Tate's corner. But luck can change in a heartbeat.

Too bad for Tate.

TWENTY-ONE

They rode off the mountain with only the stars to guide them. The air was crisp and the heavens shone brightly. Juan Escobar seemed tireless. He obviously was worried about his dogs and his flock of sheep.

"I underestimated him in every way," Clint said to the woman who rode quietly beside him, stirrup to stirrup.

"Don't feel too badly," Milly replied. "I underestimated Juan, too. After they killed his brother, he seemed to fall apart. Juan loved Miguel. The two were inseparable. Juan can't be more than seventeen."

"What are you going to do now?" Clint asked.

She looked at him a little strangely. "You think I ought to sell, don't you?"

"I think you should, yes," he told her. "Your life isn't worth losing over a piece of land."

She snorted in anger. " 'A piece of land'? Come on Clint, you must be able to understand why I can't just give in."

"Then sell to someone powerful enough to stand up to the logging interests."

Milly Turner stared right at him in the moonlight. "All right," she said, "you're the only man I know who is that strong, Clint. I want to sell half of my ranch to you."

He had not been expecting anything like this. "You're crazy! What would I want with a ranch? I'm no sheepman. I don't even know much about cattle. And as far as timber

127

and water . . . well, it just isn't my line of work."

"Make it 'your line of work,' Clint! You and I could be partners. We could save the beautiful Carson Valley from being gobbled up by special interests. And think about these mountainsides! You saw what strip-logging can do. Those mountains won't have anything on them for years and years. We owe something to this land. If we don't make a stand against the logging companies, who will?"

Clint frowned. "You seem to think that your ranch, with the Carson River running down through it, is the key."

"Of course it's the key!" Milly reached out and touched his face. "You've almost been killed because of it, and my husband was. Our place is the key, Clint. I don't mind being fair with the logging people. In fact, the rate we charge is ridiculously low. If Jeb Oatman ever gains control of the water rights, he'll choke off every small rancher and farmer between our place and Dayton. He'll ruin hundreds of families, and he'll kill the land itself for the almighty dollar. I need your help, Clint. Without you, I don't have a prayer."

"Let me think about it," he said, feeling trapped by her logic and her desperate need.

She brightened almost instantly. "Thank you!" she exclaimed. "I knew that you couldn't just walk away from me."

Clint shook his head. "You are a very persuasive woman."

"You haven't seen the half of it," she told him in a quiet, almost mysterious voice.

All the way back to the ranch, Clint wondered about that last statement. He just couldn't figure out her meaning. He was still thinking about it when she bandaged the latest wound he'd received.

"Did you see how relieved Jaun was when he saw that the flock and his dogs were just fine?" Clint asked, as they sat together before a crackling fire, both too wide awake to think of sleep.

"Yes." Milly smiled sadly. "I was pretty relieved myself. I had almost assumed that Oatman would have sent a few of his men out here to shoot or burn the flock while it was unprotected."

"Burn them?"

Milly nodded. "It's happened before. You see, sheep have lanolin in their wool and that burns like a torch. I've seen the charred bodies of sheep that have been torched. It's a terrible sight. All across the West, sheepmen have had to face long odds against cattlemen or more powerful interests."

"Ever think of raising cattle?"

"Yes, but Abner just hated them. Maybe now . . . I don't know. I've always liked cattle."

Clint nodded. "Cattle and horses are my choice. You've got a perfect location for either, and with all the water you can use to irrigate pastures, it would be my choice. I imagine there will always be a strong market on the Comstock for beef."

Milly nodded. Her face showed her growing excitement. "Of course there would be! Those miners buy all the mutton we can produce. And they like beef even more." She leaned close to the Gunsmith. "Clint, I know this sounds terrible, but . . . well, we could make a wonderful team. If we can just survive and win out over Oatman and a few of his kind, we could do anything together."

Clint took her into his arms and kissed her lips. It wasn't something he had even given a moment's thought about doing. It just happened. Maybe it was the fact that they had just gotten through a bad situation together. Or maybe it was the way that the firelight turned the edges of her hair golden. Clint didn't try to analyze it, he just wanted to take the woman into his arms and kiss her.

To his surprise, she melted eagerly against his body. She wrapped her arms around his neck and kissed him with fierce passion. "Oh," she sighed, "I feel so ashamed. I've only been a widow . . ."

Clint touched her lips with his fingers and pushed her back down on the couch. "Your husband liked and trusted me," he told the young woman. "And I liked him right away. He'd want me to help you so I guess I will."

Clint unbuttoned the man's shirt Milly wore and removed it. She began to breath heavily. Her breasts were firm, not large, but very lovely and the nipples were hard. He bent and took one into his mouth and her back arched toward him.

"Would my husband have wanted me to do this so soon?" she asked almost breathlessly.

Clint pulled back from her and stood up. He extended his hand to her, and she came to her feet very close before him. The Gunsmith reached down and unbuckled her pants, then slid his hand down over her flat belly to caress her womanhood. She began to shake and thrust her hips forward. Clint said, "Why don't we just give your husband the benefit of the doubt?"

She nodded eagerly. Her hands tore at his own belt. In a mad frenzy, they undressed each other and stood before the fire. "You're a beautiful woman, Milly Turner."

She kissed an old bullet wound on his shoulder. Kissed his broken ribs, and her lips covered his chest, neck, and face. "And you," she whispered, "have been through many wars. Your body has suffered very much."

Clint nodded. He eased her down on the couch, and she placed one bare foot on the floor, and the other she draped over the back of the couch. Just looking at her, Clint felt his manhood come to attention.

"I need a hero and you've been doing a pretty fair job of it," she said. "Heroes should be rewarded for their services, don't you agree?"

Clint stared hungrily at all that beautiful womanhood waiting for him to fill. He swallowed noisily and climbed between her widely parted legs. "Yeah, Milly, I guess they should at that."

As their lips met, Clint drove his penis into her and Milly shuddered with delight. She had long, shapely legs and the one resting on the back of the couch dropped down and over the small of his back. The one on the floor jerked up and down as he began to drive in and out of her and then it came off the floor to also lock around his back.

Outside, the sun was coming up, but as their bodies began to strain against each other, Clint knew that they would not be going anywhere this day.

He was going to buy himself a piece of Milly's ranch.

TWENTY-TWO

Two days later, Clint was working in the barn, trying to fix a busted wagon wheel, when Milly called from the house. "Riders coming!"

Clint was wearing his six-gun, and he grabbed the Winchester close at hand and stepped out into the yard. Milly also had a rifle and came to stand by his side. Clint pulled the brim of his hat down low. "Do you recognize them?"

Milly hesitated for a moment, then visibly relaxed. "Yes," she said. "It's . . . why, it's Tom Pearson, the blacksmith! And he's brought some of the ranchers and farmers from down in the valley."

"Good," Clint said. "I was wondering when some of the others who have a big stake in our survival would finally decide that they had better sit in on this card game. If we fail, so do they."

The riders galloped into the ranch yard and, except for Tom, who was grinning as if he had just found out he'd inherited money, they were a stiff and grim-faced bunch. A few of the cattlemen looked tough, but most of them appeared as you would expect small-time cattlemen and farmers to look — hard-working and frugal men who had to daily fight for a bare existence.

"Look what I brought!" Tom said as he dismounted and came forward. "I thought it was time that maybe we all started pulling together."

"You're wanted by the law," Clint said.

Pearson shrugged his muscular shoulders as if it did not

133

matter. "There's no law in Pine Bluff. Rangles is dead and Doug Ford is gone."

Milly placed her hands on her hips. "You know what the Gunsmith means," she said.

Pearson just grinned wider. "If he means Jeb Oatman and his gunnies, then I disagree entirely. Me and my friends are citizens of this here county, and I've about convinced them that I ought to be elected sheriff."

"What?"

"You heard me, Mrs. Turner, I said I am going to petition the town council of Pine Bluff for the job of sheriff. At least until they can get together and hire a better man."

Clint admired the young blacksmith's courage, but not his sense. "Tom," he said, "I don't think that you'd last very long against Oatman's hired guns. There's a man named Pickney who I know to be very fast."

"All right," the powerful young man said. "Then you petition for the job of sheriff."

Milly grabbed his arm protectively. "Clint, I don't think you'd better even think of it."

But Clint wasn't listening. "Tom, would you agree to serve as my deputy?"

"Hell, yes!" Pearson's eyes narrowed. "You serious?"

"Damn right I am." The Gunsmith studied Milly closely. "Don't you see the way of it? Even if I could get to Oatman and shoot him like he deserves, it would be declared murder. Without any proof and without authority to dig around and get proof of what's been going on in Pine Bluff, we're fighting a hopeless battle."

Milly was still not convinced. "But—"

Clint did not let her finish. "If I were the sheriff, I could do things and they'd be legal. Without that, I'd be arrested and sentenced to prison or the gallows. The deck is rigged against us in Pine Bluff."

Clint looked up at the men that Tom Pearson had brought with him. "We have to unite, and we have to go into town as a body of men determined to pressure the town council into naming me acting sheriff."

"It's a crazy idea," a rough old cattleman growled. "The town council is appointed by the logging interests. They wouldn't cut their own throats."

Clint had a ready answer. "They will if they see no alternative but to lose everything. They're the merchants, right?"

The cattlemen and farmers nodded.

"Well," Clint said. "For starters, we can threaten to buy everything from Carson City. That would hurt them in their pocketbooks. And if that isn't enough, we can remind them that once the timber is stripped from these mountainsides, the loggers will move on down the valley."

"They've already sort of done that," a farmer said. "They've started a new settlement about twenty miles south near the Walker River. They're beginning to log down there pretty heavy now."

"Well, that's the answer we use when they try to back out of supporting Tom and me," Clint said. "We hammer on that fact."

"And what if that doesn't work?"

"Then we just hammer period," he replied. "If they're so short-sighted that they can't see a yard into their futures, they need educating. But it will take all of us working together."

"Might work," the cattleman said.

"Might, hell!" Tom Pearson said roughly. "It has to work! Like each and every man here, I've got a lifetime investment tied up in my stable. I'm not going to let that business go to hell. I'll fight, and I suspect that once the town council gets to thinking about that little settlement down on the Walker River, they'll come to their senses and fight, too!"

Clint agreed. He looked into the faces of these men and he saw hard times and worry lines. There was no need to tell them that they were up against a powerful group of men who would ruthlessly take advantage of their every weakness. To Clint's way of thinking, Jeb Oatman was the key, and to get to him, Clint figured he'd have to go through the gunfighter named Pickney.

"Let's get started," Clint said. "We're all together and there's no sense in waiting any longer."

The men looked at each other and one of them, a farmer in his mid-fifties with silver hair, said in a hopeful voice, "Tom Pearson said you were the fastest man alive with a six-gun. Is that true?"

"Probably not," Clint said, not wanting anyone to depend on him too much. If he were gunned down, he'd want Pearson to step forward and lead these men. "I am handy with guns and I have fought a few men."

"Few men!" Pearson shouted. "Why, when I was in Carson City, I asked about you and they—"

Clint's voice hardened. "What is in the past is in the past, Tom. Every man, sooner or later, meets a better man."

"You killed Rangles, didn't you?"

"I did."

"And what about Elvis Tate?"

The Gunsmith looked at Milly. He did not want to relate the whole story. How she'd been abducted and forced to spend several days with three of Oatman's gunmen. Milly hadn't spoken of it, and Clint had no intention of asking her what had happened while she had been in that mountain cabin.

"I shot Tate, but I had some help. But again, that's in the past."

The same farmer shuffled his feet in the dirt and said, "Maybe it is in the past and you don't want to talk about it, Gunsmith. But the fact is, Rangles and Tate were fast on the trigger and you killed 'em both. That means that the rest of the snakes in Oatman's den are wiggling their rattles a little faster and they'll think twice about bracing you."

Clint decided that this was a good time to set things straight. "Understand me well," he said, addressing them all. "Before we ride into Pine Bluff to make a stand, you have to understand that the success or failure of what we do does not solely depend on me—or Tom or Milly Turner. It depends on each one of us. We're fighting together, but each one of you is also fighting for your own livelihood. There'll be no backing up if things go hard for us. Is that understood?"

They nodded solemnly.

"Then let's ride," Clint said.

"I'm coming, too," Milly told him.

"I never expected for a single minute that you wouldn't," the Gunsmith told her.

He and Tom watched Milly head for the barn. Even in a man's Levi's and shirt, she still looked mighty inviting and there was no hiding the nice curves of her body. Tom Pearson must have thought so, too, for he said, "You and her, you're sort of. . . ."

"Sort of in this thing together," Clint said, "just like we all are."

Pearson scowled. "You know that's not what I meant."

Clint looked at the tall young blacksmith and it was plain to see that the man was in love with Milly and probably had been for many years. "Tom, when this is all over, I'll either be planted under the ground or I'll be riding my horse on over to San Francisco—after you shoe the animal. Either way, I won't be hanging around Milly Turner. Does that answer your question?"

"Yes, it does," Pearson said, unable to keep the relief out of his voice. "It sure as hell does!"

TWENTY-THREE

It was late afternoon when they rode into Pine Bluff, and Clint directed the men who rode with him to bring the town council members together for an emergency meeting. Milly helped draw up the list and assigned three riders to each council member.

"They ain't going to want to come," a rancher said. "Especially Zeb Cather and Archibald MacDonald. They'll fight like hell."

"I can handle Zeb Cather," Tom Pearson said. "I whipped him when we were kids, I can do it again if necessary."

Clint suppressed a smile. "Milly, why don't you tag along with Tom and try to keep things peaceable between Cather and Tom. There's no sense bringing in a man that's beat to a bloody pulp. Maybe you can charm the man into our way of thinking."

"What about you?" she asked, clearly not wanting to leave his side.

"I'll pay a visit to that Archibald MacDonald fella. Where can I find him?"

"He owns the gun shop right down the street," Milly said. "And he isn't above demonstrating his wares at the slightest opportunity."

"I'll keep that in mind," the Gunsmith said as he headed off down the street.

When he came to the gun shop, Clint stepped inside. Being a gunsmith himself, he thoroughly enjoyed visiting other gunsmiths and seeing the quality of their work.

"What do you need?" a small man with a bulldog's jaw and pugnacious manner snapped.

Clint studied the firearms that MacDonald had on display. There was an entire glass case filled with guns of every description, from the old flintlocks to pepperboxes to a wide assortment of derringers. Mostly, though, Clint saw Colt .45s and Smith & Wessons but he also saw a .44 caliber Remington New Model Army pistol that was a beauty.

"Rifles in the rack are all under fifty dollars," MacDonald said, barely looking up from his workbench where he was repairing a Buffalo Rifle.

"What about this one?" Clint asked, pointing to a Winchester Model 1873 that had been reworked and reblued. The stock had been custom-made and hand-polished to a high shine. "What kind of wood is this?"

"Oak," MacDonald said, almost defensively. "It's hard to work with, but I like the way the grain shows through after it's finished.

"Oak. Well, I'll be damned. First time I ever saw a stock made out of that kind of wood."

"That's because few men have the patience or skill that I do when it comes to building a new stock."

Clint nodded. It was clear that Archibald MacDonald wasn't suffering from inferiority and that the man was blunt and very prideful when it came to his own gunsmithing ability. "You're a master craftsman, Mr. MacDonald," Clint said. "No question in my mind about that. This Winchester is a work of art," Clint told the little gunsmith. "Mind if I handle it?"

MacDonald sized Clint up. "You look like the sort of a man who knows weapons. Sure. Go ahead."

Clint took the rifle and tested its balance. "Perfect," he said, hefting it to his shoulder. This was the .44-40 with twelve shots in a twenty-inch barrel that was strong and yet light. "A rifle like this is hard to find."

MacDonald nodded. "It's the best I've ever done. I wouldn't take any less than three hundred dollars for it. Not a cent. And I've been offered two-fifty many times."

"It's easy to see why. A man could travel the world and not find a better weapon. With forty grains of powder behind each slug, this honey will knock down a grizzly bear at fifty yards."

"It's an Indian killer, for sure," MacDonald said, his reserve melting like butter in a hot skillet. "I been thinking that Buffalo Bill Cody would buy it if he seen it. You know, it's his favorite of the Winchesters. I hear he owns a good half-dozen of them and swears that there is nothing better for all-around hunting."

"Well, I sure would agree with you on that," Clint said. He studied the rifle. He had a Winchester 1866 that he had customized for his own purposes and it was a beauty. But this weapon was even finer. Maybe three hundred dollars was stretching things a little, but not a great deal. Besides, if it bought a vote for his becoming sheriff from this crusty little town council member, Clint figured it would be worth that alone. Now came the hard part. Clint knew it was time to make his sales pitch and see how MacDonald reacted. He'd warmed him up with a bunch of compliments, but getting the prickly little fella to commit to something like voting for him was another matter entirely, and Clint needed to find out where the man stood.

"Do you know who I am?"

"Nope." MacDonald snapped his suspenders. "I make it a habit never to pry into a man's affairs."

"My name is Clint Adams." Clint placed the rifle down on the counter.

MacDonald nodded, his face losing its friendliness. "You're the man who killed Deputy Rangles and took up with the Turners."

"That's right. But I killed Rangles in self-defense."

"You did Pine Bluff a favor," MacDonald admitted. "I couldn't stand the bastard. He was always hanging around my shop, bragging about his gun speed."

Clint said, "He was fast, but he was a man without honor.

Pine Bluff would have suffered under him if he'd have been appointed sheriff."

"We're better off without him or Doug Ford," MacDonald said.

"But we do need a sheriff," Clint said. "As you well know, Mrs. Turner's husband was gunned down in the street by a man named Elvis Tate. Some innocent woman or child might have been shot to death by accident."

"Abner Turner was a fool to come into Pine Bluff."

"This was his town as much as any man's," Clint argued. "Abner's father was one of the first settlers. As for the gunfight itself, I saw it but was helpless to stop the murder. Elvis Tate is dead now; he tried to kill me, too."

"Tate is dead?"

"Yes." Clint set the Winchester down. "I was lucky enough to kill him, too. Jeb Oatman and his kind are running scared. Mr. MacDonald, Pine Bluff is a fine town, a family town that has been taken over by the big logging interests. We aim to change that. This town needs law, and I want to be the one that cleans it up."

MacDonald shook his head. "You'll never get anywhere in Pine Bluff, unless it's a free ride to the cemetery."

"I think you're wrong. We want you to attend an emergency town council meeting in less than an hour, and I want you to vote for me as your acting sheriff."

MacDonald laughed right out loud. "Now why should I do a crazy thing like that!"

Clint told the man. Told him how all the small farmers and ranchers were banding together and how they were going to fight with their buying power and their guns, if necessary.

MacDonald wasn't impressed. "Hell," he snapped. "They never buy much of anything from me anyway."

"And neither will the logging people when they've stripped the forests above Pine Bluff and gone elsewhere with their business. Besides that, you ever seen real floods? I have. What do you think is going to keep all the soil up on the mountainside above town once it has been stripped of trees?"

MacDonald blinked, and it seemed clear that he had not considered the possibility of flooding. Before he could formulate some rebuttal, Clint said, "I'm told that there's already a new town south of here. That's where the logging is going to go. It'll be closer to a big river, the Walker."

"I don't believe it," MacDonald said.

"Oh, it'll happen if the logging interests get control of Milly Turner's ranch and then strip the forest away and send it all down the Carson River. If that happens, Pine Bluff will be nothing but a mudslide in five years."

"I helped found this town," MacDonald said.

"So did Milly's family—and Abner's, too. They built it to last, not to be raped by special-interest loggers who don't give a damn about anything but the dollars in their pockets. Think about it for a moment, Mr. MacDonald. It's not the logging people that will remain and build, it's the ranchers and the farmers that sink roots instead of tearing them up. Pine Bluff can last and be a monument to people like you, or it can drown in mud and greed. It's your choice. I've sort of been shoveled into the forefront of this thing, and I'm willing to accept the job of acting sheriff."

"We do need law, if it was honest and had enough guts to stand up to the hooligans in this town," MacDonald said. "Every night there are shootings and stabbings. The loggers get drunk and act like animals. I can't trust my wife and daughters out after dark anymore. It's gotten out of hand. I tell you!"

"Sure, it has. And I've been a sheriff for years. There's going to be trouble at first, but"—Clint delivered his final pitch—"with a fine rifle like this and plenty of support from men like you and Tom Pearson, I expect we can work together and turn things around."

MacDonald had small but powerful hands. Almost unconsciously, they stroked the smooth oak stock of the Winchester with loving affection. He took a deep breath and looked the Gunsmith squarely in the eye and said, "Three hundred dollars might be a little high," he admitted. "I might let it go to someone famous such as yourself for two seventy-five."

"Sold!" Clint said, sticking out his hand.

Archibald MacDonald stuck his own hand out. "Gunsmith, you got my rifle and you got my vote! I'll back you and Tom right down the line."

They shook hands on the deal. Clint had to go to the bank just before it closed and withdraw the cash, but it was as good a use for money as a man could ever find. He just hoped that Tom Pearson and the others were finding things as easy.

TWENTY-FOUR

Milly Turner had known Tom Pearson since they were children. To her, Tom had always been a tall, gawky, and very skinny boy with pimples and a cowlick that stood up as high as a rooster's tail. As early as ten years of age, Milly was aware that Tom used to follow her around when she came to town, kind of like a puppy. Once, when she was fourteen, she had whirled, caught him by surprise, and made a truly horrible face at him. He'd flushed and ran. Milly always remembered the humiliated expression she'd seen on Tom's face as he realized he was being mocked. After that, Tom Pearson had not followed her again, and she discovered that she had missed his doting attention.

Tom's father had been a drunk and a hell-raiser. Tom's mother had been a Christian woman and the town had thought of her almost as a martyr for putting up with Hench Pearson. Milly recalled stories about Hench Pearson's all-night drinking bouts, how he almost burned down his own stable one night in a drunken rage and how he used to beat his son whenever he was able to lay hands on him. Sober, Hench Pearson had been just tolerable; drunk, he had been a nightmarish figure, brawling, swearing, half-crazed, and filled with hatred. Milly did not know for sure, but she always was a little afraid that Tom would inherit his father's love for the bottle and his wild and tormented personality.

But Tom had escaped Pine Bluff at fifteen to become a prospector in the California gold country. Ten years later, when Milly was engaged to Abner Turner, Tom Pearson had trooped back over the Sierras and visited her ranch. He had changed dramatically. No longer was he either skinny or pimply. In fact, he was a big, ruggedly handsome, broad-shouldered young man standing well over six feet tall. And he was obviously still very much in love with her. When Milly had told him about her engagement to Abner, she had seen pain in his eyes, and he had left soon after that but not before giving her a little gold pendant from the gold fields.

For a while, Tom had worked on the Comstock Lode in a blacksmith shop. He had frequently visited his mother, whose health had rapidly failed. A year earlier, Hench Pearson had gotten drunk and been kicked to death by a mule while pinned in a stall. Tom's mother had died just six weeks later. Tom had come back to Pine Bluff and taken over his father's livery. And then, he had been chased out by the logging people after the Gunsmith's arrival in town.

Zeb Cather owned the feed store, and he was out on an errand when they arrived at his establishment. There was nothing to do but take a seat on a bale of hay and wait for his return.

Tom was quiet. He chewed reflectively on a blade of al-falfa and studied his big, callused hands. "I was mighty sorry about your husband," he said quietly. "Abner was a good man and I liked and respected him a lot."

Milly looked over at him. "He liked you, Tom."

"Did he ever. . . ." Tom struggled for the right words. "Did you ever tell him about how I used to follow you around all the time?"

"He knew about it. The whole town did," Milly said. "I never told you how sorry I was about making that awful face."

"I had it coming."

"No, you didn't!" Milly reached out and placed her hand on his muscular shoulder. "It was a shameful thing for me to do. I've never forgiven myself for being so cruel."

"Aw, any girl would get sick of some ugly kid following her around like a dog or something. I was just so . . . so damned smitten over you. I guess I always have been, Milly."

"I can't imagine why," she told him. "I'm not an easy person to live with. Not at all. I'm not a good cook, or even a good housekeeper. Mostly, I care about my sheep and shepherds and the dogs. I'd rather be outdoors on a horse or walking with the sheep than penned up inside a house. I'd make a terrible mother, and—"

"Stop it," he said, a little abruptly. "I never figured you for a saint. You know my own background. I might go crazy when I hit thirty-five just the same way my father did. To this very day I won't even have a beer 'cause I'm so afraid of winding up like him. Some people say I will, you know. They say I'll be ten times worse because I'm a lot bigger and stronger than Pa was. And I guess if I did go crazy and start fighting, I'd probably kill or at least hurt some poor fella real bad. I'd want someone to shoot me as if I was rabid."

Tom nodded his head as if he had just convinced himself of the logic of his own violent demise. "Yes, ma'am, that'd be the best thing for everyone."

Milly realized that tears were clouding her vision. "Tom, don't say that to me. If someone shot you, I'd feel as if something special in my life had died," she managed to say.

He looked up. "You really mean that?"

She nodded. "I do. You're one of the last people I know I could trust. One of the only ones left."

"What about Clint Adams?"

"I guess I love him, too," she said. "In fact, I know I do. But he's not fooling me. He'll move on when this trouble is over. And then, I'll be alone."

"No you won't. I'll be here. If I don't get killed, I'll always be around to help you, Milly. I swear that I will!"

Milly looked at him closely. "I don't understand what you think is so special about me, Tom. Even when we were children, the thing that bothered me most of all wasn't that you followed me around. Heck, no! That was flattering. The thing that made me troubled was the fear that you and I. . . . Well, you'd really get to know me and then you'd realize that you'd been following an illusion. Someone who really had only existed in your mind."

Tom reached out and pulled her into his arms, and before Milly realized it, he kissed her and she kissed him back. Tom released her and jumped off the bale of hay and said, "That's no illusion, Milly. And neither are you. I'll say one more thing, and then I'll shut up because I probably have said way too much already. I loved you the first time I saw you and I never got over it. I'll always think of you as my girl. And when this trouble is past, I'll ask you to marry me. And I'll tell the Gunsmith that face-to-face."

Tom clamped his mouth shut. He had just made the longest speech of his life, and he guessed he'd gotten in all the things he'd wanted to say for so many years. And so now, if he wound up getting shot by one of Oatman's gunfighters, at least he wouldn't have gone to his grave without even having the nerve to proclaim his love.

Zeb Cather was their age, but he looked fifteen years older. He had put on a lot of lard around the middle. His face was slack and his eyes bloodshot from the whiskey he consumed after work each evening. He was a nondescript-looking man, except for the intense weariness in his face. He was also a pessimist who never took chances except when he was provoked or his quick temper got the better of him. He was a member of the town council of Pine Bluff, and he liked to talk to hear the wisdom of his own words, but few people cared to listen. Zeb was unpopular, but he owned the only feed store in town and for that reason alone, he had managed to earn a decent living.

He took one look at big Tom Pearson and said, "I thought

they run you off somewhere. I was wanting to buy your stable."

"No chance," Tom said. "I'm back to stay."

Cather did not look pleased. "Maybe you ought to rethink it, Tom. I'd give you five hundred dollars for your business. It's worthless to you now."

Milly had heard enough. She had also been forced to use Zeb Cather's feed store for years, just like Abner and their parents had used it. "Tom and I are both standing up against Jeb Oatman and his men. You know who the Gunsmith is, don't you?"

"Yeah," Cather said. "I know how you and your late husband hired him to fight Oatman and the logging interests. It was a mistake."

"No, it wasn't," Milly argued. "Tom and the other small ranchers and farmers have banded together and come to town. We're calling a special meeting of the Pine Bluff town council in order to get the Gunsmith appointed as our sheriff."

"You're out of your mind!"

Tom moved forward, big hands ready to grab Cather by the throat. Milly just managed to throw herself in front of Tom and prevent a disaster. There was little question that Cather wasn't half man enough anymore to whip Tom, but he was mulishly stubborn and beating or choking him was exactly the wrong approach to take if you needed his cooperation.

"Zeb, listen to me! We're going to elect the Gunsmith with or without your vote. We can get enough votes from the town councilmen to do the job."

"So why are you here, then!" Cather said sarcastically. "If you don't need my vote, then get along and leave me to my business."

Tom took a deep breath and let it out slowly. "Think about it," he said. "Who brings you business? Do the logging interests buy much hay and grain, or is it people like me and the small ranchers and farmers? Zeb, we've agreed to go to Carson City for our hay and grain if you won't help us right now."

"Carson City! Hell, Tom, that would add another dollar a ton in freight charges on hay and grain. You want to throw away good money on higher prices for feed, I say go ahead."

Milly knew the man was bluffing. She could see a seed of worry in his bloodshot eyes. "Zeb, we could also open a cooperative feed store of our own. Hire a manager and probably drive you out of business in three months, six at the most."

Now Zeb Cather really began to see the light. He pulled his dirty bandanna out of his back pocket and blew his nose. "You folks have supported me real good through the years," he conceded. "I don't want to lose your loyalty."

"Well, you will," Tom growled, pressing their shifting advantage hard now. "If you don't show up at the town hall and vote for the Gunsmith for sheriff and me for his deputy, I'll be buying you out for five hundred dollars."

Cather ran his fingers through his thinning gray hair. "Your father was a sonofabitch, everyone knows that, but he bought a hell of a lot of hay and grain from me for many years."

"I know that, Zeb. And so will Milly and I if you stand with us on this thing. We need men like you with enough guts and determination to turn this town around. Make it decent again. I hope you decide to go with us. If not, we'll bury this business in six months, and that's a promise."

Tom took Milly's arm and escorted her out toward the street.

"Hey, wait a minute!" Cather shouted, following them. "What if you and the Gunsmith both get shot to death? Me and the rest of the council members will be up to our necks in trouble."

"That's right," Tom said. "Your vote is just the start. If fighting comes, you'll all have to choose sides. Choose ours, Zeb. I promise you, we are going to win."

Zeb nodded. "I think you might at that," he said. "In fact, I know you will. Tom, I'll be there!"

Milly hugged Tom Pearson's arm. "You were terrific!" she said. "I never imagined you could be that persuasive. The way you talked, he had to say yes."

Tom smiled. "If you think I was persuasive back there, just wait until this is over and I ask you to marry me."

TWENTY-FIVE

When Clint entered the meeting room, he found himself immediately engulfed in raging controversy and mass confusion. There were at least fifty people crowded into the little room that had been built to handle no more than thirty.

"Clint!" Milly shouted, beckoning him toward her and Tom Pearson. "Over here!"

Clint pushed his way through the crowd and reached her side. The din was so loud that Milly had to shout to be heard. "Oatman and the logging people got word of this and some of them are in the room fomenting trouble for us."

"Point them out to me!"

Milly pointed them out. Clint grabbed Tom's arm and said, "They'll be watching me closely. When I approach Pickney, you move in behind and grab him around the arms. Don't—under any circumstances—let the man reach for his six-gun. In a room this packed, it would set off a panic, and some innocent bystander would almost certainly be killed."

Tom nodded. "We're going right after Pickney, huh?"

"Yep. It's my experience that, if you kick the meanest dog in the butt, the others will generally chase after him with their tails between their legs."

"Let's go, then," Tom said, worry plainly written on his face.

Clint watched Tom ease into the crowd. He could see Pickney and the rest were watching him very closely, and he waited until Tom managed to position himself where he would be able to grab the head gunman.

"Be careful," Milly said.

"I will. I don't think Pickney is so stupid as to open fire in a room of people. He knows that it would backfire and create a stampede in which he might get trampled along with everyone else. But we'll see."

Clint started forward, and now every eye in the room was on him. Men squeezed out of his way and when they saw that he was going right for Pickney, they shoved hard to clear an open path between the two dangerous gunfighters. Some of them panicked and tried to crowd out of the door, but most grabbed the butts of their own guns and waited to see what might happen.

Clint stopped just five feet in front of the gunman. "I don't think we want you and your friends in this meeting hall," he said. "It's sort of invitation only. Understand?"

Pickney grinned. "This is a public place. I'm a member of the public and so are my friends. I think we'll stay."

"No, you won't."

Pickney had not expected the Gunsmith to force a show-down in such a bad situation. He hid his surprise well, however, and like a professional, he was ready. "I guess you and I had better settle this issue right here and now, Gunsmith. I always wondered if I could beat a real legend."

At that moment, Tom Pearson lunged at Pickney and his powerful arms clamped the man's arms to his sides. Pickney was not a big man and when he struggled, Tom gave him such a bear hug that his face drained of blood and he looked as if he were going to explode.

In the meantime, Clint had drawn his gun and now the barrel of his Colt was aimed loosely at the other gunmen who had been caught flatfooted in surprise at this unexpected turn of events. "You boys had better reach around with your off hands and unbuckle your guns and let them drop to the floor."

The gunmen did not argue. They dropped their guns and holsters.

"Now," Clint said. "Just walk out of this room nice and easy. Tell Jeb Oatman and his cronies that, if they try anything more, I'll be around to pay them a visit."

One of the gunman said, "What about Pickney?"

Clint looked at the man. He appeared ready to faint. "Why don't someone take his gun and we'll let him go before he suffers any permanent brain damage."

Pickney was disarmed, and Tom dropped him like a sack of flour. The man collapsed on the floor and gasped for breath. He was as white as the belly of a beached catfish and about as comfortable.

"Why don't a few of you good men carry him outside where he can get some fresh air," Clint said.

There was no shortage of helping hands. Pickney was despised and feared and they tossed him unceremoniously out in the street and slammed the door behind him. Several of the small ranchers stood guard beside the door to make certain that there were no more unwelcome intruders.

All eyes were on Clint now, and with the ejection of Pickney and his friends, he could almost feel the mounting optimism and excitement. It had been years since anyone had dared to stand up to Oatman or his gunmen and now, in just a matter of a few minutes, the Gunsmith and Tom Pearson had sent them all packing.

Clint cleared his voice and said, "Citizens of Pine Bluff. I guess we have a quorum of voting members of the town council here now. And I know that everyone in this room understands why this meeting was called and what I hope will come of it. This town is too fine a place to be strangled to death by the interests of just a few. What Mrs. Turner and Tom Pearson and the rest of us want is simple justice. We think all the citizens of Pine Bluff have an interest in those mountains right above us. And we know that, if they are picked clean, this valley will be ruined forever and Pine Bluff will be no more. If you elect me sheriff, and Tom Pearson as my deputy, we'll try and see that things change for the better."

"What are you going to do to stay alive?" one of the people shouted. "Oh, sure, we got the drop on Pickney and a couple of them. But this town is overrun by loggers and they know who pays their wages. Besides that, there's a lot more men on Oatman's payroll than we've seen so far."

Clint nodded. He had expected exactly this kind of questioning, and it sounded just like the fears he had heard dozens of times in his lifetime. Getting townspeople to understand that, sometimes, they might have to fight to save what mattered most was never easy.

"If every single man in this room is willing to stand up for what he believes in, we can win this thing without a single bullet being fired," Clint told them. "Once Jeb Oatman and his kind understand that we will not be intimidated, bullied, or bought off, they'll back down."

"Of course they will!" Milly cried. "My father was murdered and so was my husband. What makes any of you think that it couldn't happen to yourselves? You don't have any choice but to fight."

"We're not fighters, we're a bunch of gray-haired merchants!" a butcher shop owner yelled.

Clint nodded. "As I said, if you appoint me and Tom as sheriff and deputy—then stand behind us no matter what—we can lick them without firing a shot. But if you don't, I guarantee that you'll not be making a living in Pine Bluff within three years from now."

Tom echoed that sentiment. "You folks may not like the term, but what we have here is a war—with logging on one side, and all the rest of us on the other. We either fight, or we'll be ground under. So which is it?"

A cheer started and then grew to a hoarse roar as the citizens of Pine Bluff raised their closed fists in a token salute.

"I think the town council is going to vote us in!" Tom yelled to the Gunsmith.

Clint nodded. The issue was no longer in doubt.

TWENTY-SIX

Clint and Tom were unanimously voted into office and Archibald MacDonald, who also served as the mayor of the town, pinned the badges on their chests. It was a great moment for the Gunsmith; for the first time, he figured that things were going to change in Pine Bluff.

"All right," he yelled, "we're going over to face Oatman and his men and set down the law. I want everyone behind me."

Clint, Milly, and Tom headed for the door and the fired-up crowd followed. Zeb Cather and the little gunsmith, MacDonald, were right there, striding step for step as they marched down Main Street toward the offices of Sierra Timber.

But when they rounded a corner, they suddenly came into full view of about forty burly loggers. They were carrying axe-handles and rifles and they were fronted by Pickney and at least six other hired gunmen. Clint felt an ice-ball form in his stomach. He did not break stride, but he could almost feel the merchants behind him begin to break away from him and scatter down the alleyways.

"The chicken-hearted cowards are deserting us like rats from a sinking ship!" Tom choked in anger.

Clint said, "Milly, why don't you—"

"Don't even suggest such a thing!" she snapped.

Clint swore in helpless anger. He would be a fool if he thought he could outgun Pickney and almost a dozen hand-picked shooters. And even if they could get past them somehow, what about all those loggers? Why, they looked ready to go on a rampage and destroy the town, if given the slightest provocation.

"What are we going to do?" Tom asked.

"Bluff them," Clint said.

"Bluff 'em!" Tom could not believe his ears. "Look around behind us, man!"

Clint looked over his shoulder. Where they had left the meeting hall with over thirty, there were now less than ten, and they certainly were no match for the men up ahead.

"That's far enough!" Pickney yelled.

Clint kept walking. He could feel the sweat break out across his body, and he wondered if this was the end of the line for him. If so, he'd had his share of this world, lots of beautiful women, good friends, and a fine horse. He'd saved many lives and taken just as many bad ones. All in all, it was not a bad record he'd compiled.

But what about Milly Turner and a young man like Tom Pearson? Hell, they'd scarcely begun to live.

Cling took eight more strides and then he stopped in his tracks. He saw Oatman, who stood slightly to the left of his men, among three of his cronies. The Gunsmith focused his attention on the four wealthy logging men. He carried his new Winchester in his left hand and his right hand was very near to the butt of his gun.

"Oatman, you and your friends are finished in Pine Bluff."

Oatman laughed out loud. "Look behind you again, Gunsmith. Hell, your new friends just ran out on you. That badge you and Pearson are wearing ain't no more than a target now."

"Maybe."

"Mrs. Turner, you're a beautiful, if foolish, young woman. Please step off the street to safety. I don't want to see you hurt."

"Go to hell!" Milly cried.

"I'm sorry you feel that way," the logging man said. "I'm afraid this is going to be a slaughter."

"If it is," Clint said, "it will be on your conscience. Tell your men to disperse. I'm the law now, and I demand that these gunfighters of yours hand over their weapons at once."

But Oatman shook his head. He and three other expensively dressed men turned and headed back for the offices. Clint did not have a clean shot or he might have decided to take them out once and for all.

When Oatman and his friends were safely inside, Pickney turned to his men. "On the count of three, we open fire! Is that clear?"

"Oh, my God!" Zeb Cather cried just before his nerve broke, and he dashed for cover. He was not alone. Clint heard a stampede of running footsteps and when he turned around, only MacDonald stood firm.

"I'm the mayor," the short man snapped. "And I don't like to see my town filled with vermin."

Clint had heard that the little gunsmith could shoot very well and now he also knew that MacDonald had a lot of courage. But courage wasn't going to get them out of this mess alive. They were trapped in a no-win situation.

Suddenly, everyone heard a shot from inside the Sierra Timber offices. It was followed by angry shouts and, a moment later, two more shots in rapid sucession. Pickney wanted to turn and dash back through the loggers to protect his employer, but he could not dare to take his attention from Clint.

The front door of the offices banged open and the wealthy logging men who had been with Oatman only moments before came flying outside. One screamed, "There's a woman in there and she's shot Jeb!"

Now Pickney backed up quickly and shouted, "Everyone stand still and don't take your eyes off these men!"

Pickney swung around and charged up on the front porch. He was right at the doorway when a shot sent him leaping sideways. Clint saw the man jump to a window, kick in the glass, and then bat the curtains aside and trigger three fast shots into the interior of the room.

"Who is it?" Milly cried.

Clint reached for Milly, but she was already running toward the building. The gunmen and the loggers parted for her and Pickney stood beside the window as if he were a block of frozen ice. Milly disappeared inside.

"That woman has a lot of guts," Tom said.

Clint nodded. "And so does the one that tried to kill Oatman and died saving our lives."

A few tense moments later, Milly stepped out on the porch. "It's a girl named Dora," she called. "She died in my arms, saying she didn't want you killed, Clint!"

Milly buried her head in her hands and cried.

The Gunsmith felt as if a tub of cold water had been thrown in his face. He felt like his insides had been kicked out. Clint handed Tom his new Winchester and started walking forward. Not giving a damn. Waiting and wanting something to happen so that he could release the anger that raged inside and threatened to kill him.

"Pickney!" he shouted, "turn and face me, you woman-killer!"

Pickney turned and said in a tight voice, "This is just me and him, everybody. Just me and the Gunsmith."

Clint made the loggers part and when he was in range, he stopped and his hand hovered over his gun. He did not wait for Pickney to start the play. Instead, his hand flashed down and the Colt in his holster jumped as if it were a live thing. Pickney was lightning fast, too. He started less than a hundredth of a second late and that was just how it ended as the gun in Clint's fist bucked and a bullet streaked to Pickney's heart.

Pickney's gun had cleared leather, but it was still pointing down when the man pulled the trigger. A stray bullet bit into the street, richocheted, and hit a logger in the leg. But Clint wasn't aware of that. He unleashed three more slugs and each one of them rocked the gunfighter back until the man's arms extended wide and he crashed backward through the glass window he had already busted.

Clint holstered his gun. His expression was bleak and murderous as he stepped up onto the porch and then entered the offices. The first thing he saw was Oatman over against one wall, ashen and moaning. But then Clint looked down at Dora with three bullet holes in her breast.

"The murdering sonofabitch!" he choked in helpless rage. Clint bent down and picked up the saloon girl and walked past Milly and out into the street. No man would shoot another carrying a dead woman. Clint didn't care one way or the other as he slowly carried Dora up Main Street to the undertaker's.

And behind him, the stunned loggers shook their heads and walked away. There would be no war this day. Not after the shocking events which had just transpired. Oatman was wounded badly and Pickney had been outdrawn and gunned down.

The logging interests had taken a beating instead of inflicting the final victory that had seemed so assured. And why? The answer was that a saloon girl had loved the Gunsmith enough to die saving his life.

TWENTY-SEVEN

Jeb Oatman tossed down another glass of expensive whiskey and grimaced as the doctor finished bandaging up his wounds. "This should never have happened to me," he gritted. "Pickney failed to protect me and so did the others. As soon as this is over, I plan to get rid of the whole bunch of them!"

Dr. William B. Cutter shook his head like a wise old sage. He was in his sixties, and the only medicine he had practiced for five years was on logging men. With Jeb Oatman as his front, Dr. Cutter quietly controlled every logging decision made on the eastern slopes of the Sierras. Dr. Cutter lived on the mountainside and his huge log cabin was a veritable fortress, one patrolled by men and dogs.

Doc Cutter had long white hair and a matching goatee. Tall, refined, and slow to speak, he looked entirely benevolent. In fact, he was the most ruthless man Jeb Oatman had ever known, and the only one he feared.

"That's poor thinking, Jeb. What you need to do is to find someone who is clever enough to kill the Gunsmith. You've tried matching guns against guns, it hasn't worked. What you need to do now is to resort to something more innovative."

"Such as?"

The doctor shrugged. "I think we ought to find someone who is capable of killing both the Gunsmith and Tom Pearson in a manner that they least expect."

"I'm listening, Doc." Oatman shook his head. "Everything I've tried has failed. What do you suggest now?"

Doc Cutter finished his work and eyed the bandaging with a professional eye. "You are very fortunate that I was close or you'd have bled to death. This will teach you to consort with a woman of dubious character that is in love with your opposition."

"I didn't know she still gave a damn about the Gunsmith! Hell, I gave Dora everything she wanted. I was good to her and she even promised to keep me informed about Clint Adams."

The doctor shook his head. "Instead of using her, she was using you. You can't afford to make that kind of mistake, Jeb. Beautiful women are your Achilles heel; they always have been."

Oatman nodded with bitterness. Doc Cutter was right. He was always right. "I've run out of ideas."

"Then ask me for your help, Jeb."

Oatman clamped his jaws together, hating the way that the doc always made a man get down on his knees and beg.

"Say it, Jeb. Humility is a virtue. Say, 'Please help me, Dr. Cutter. I need your help very much.' "

Oatman swallowed the bile that rose in his throat. "Please help me, Dr. Cutter. I need your help very much."

The doctor smiled. "Splendid! See how much better it feels to admit your weaknesses and turn to a superior mind?"

Once again, the younger man realized with certainty that he wanted to kill this twisted doctor. Cutter was crazed by the need to control other men, and he was definitely a genius but also definitely crazy. Someday, I will kill him, Oatman promised himself once more, but not until I get through this Gunsmith business.

"If you have a suggestion on how to get rid of the Gunsmith, I wish you'd just tell me," Oatman said with mounting exasperation.

"All right. Let's do something he'll never expect."

"Like what?"

The doctor smiled. "I'm a chemist and a physician. I'll

find a way to poison the man."

Something churned in the pit of Oatman's stomach. "Poison him?"

"Yes, why not?"

"I don't know," Oatman admitted. "It's just—"

"Yes," Cutter said, seeming to read his mind. "It is a terrible, really ghastly, kind of death. Very, very painful but entirely effective and very often used, though, and it was highly popular in medieval times. But if it bothers you, I suggest that you first offer a bounty on the Gunsmith. Make it enticing. Make it a thousand dollars for him, five hundred for the deputy. If that fails to achieve our intended results, then we poison him in a café or some place where he eats. We pay a cook or a waitress. It will really be quite an easy thing to do."

"I don't know," Oatman said. "The poisoning thing seems risky. It's not something I think we ought to do except as an absolute last resort. It just isn't my style. I think one of the boys will be able to kill him if the price is right."

"Come, come!" the doctor said in a reproving voice. "Surely you can't be getting squeamish."

"I just think that . . . if we took out the Gunsmith, all the others would crumble. We'd have the Turner Ranch within a month."

"Do you honestly believe that Mrs. Turner will ever sell us her ranch and water rights?"

Oatman shook his head. "No, I guess she wouldn't."

"Are you aware that, in the event of her death, Mrs. Turner has willed her ranch to be sold to the Territory of Nevada with the stipulation that the timber stands we desire not be sold for at least fifty years?"

Oatman looked up suddenly. "No, but that. . . ."

"And also," the doctor continued, "that the Territory agree to double the rate of our logs that float across her ranch property?"

"Can she do that?"

"I don't think so," the doctor said. "But even if it did

prove illegal in a court of law, Mrs. Turner has thoughtfully
provided that the ranch be given to the Brothers and Sisters
of Charity Foundation with the same conditions to apply.
And that is definitely legal."

"How do you know all this?"

Dr. Cutter looked pleased with himself. "One of my own
men in Carson City who works in the Recorder's Office
intercepted the will. Naturally, he never filed it properly."

"But Miles Ebert would raise hell if we. . . ."

The doctor nodded. "Exactly. So the first thing to do is
to kill that lawyer of hers and then insert a new will which
will sell the Turner Ranch to us for a sum of . . . oh, let's
be generous enough to avoid any accusations. Let's buy it
for ten thousand dollars."

Oatman was surprised. "When we could have it for half
that much without raising a stir?"

"I think so," Cutter said. "If we pay top dollar, then who
can accuse us of any complicity in Mrs. Turner's death?
It's good business. The timber alone on the ranch is worth
many times that amount, and we'll up the rates on the water
charges."

Oatman took a deep breath. "You really have this whole
thing figured out, don't you?"

"Yes, I do," the doctor said. "We are playing to win.
The key is to eliminate the opposition. It requires major
surgery. But first, we need a force of gunmen. Offer the
bounty and let's see if we get lucky."

Oatman hoped they did get lucky. He wasn't a bit squeamish, but he sure didn't like the idea of poisoning. Not one
damn bit, he didn't. "Tell me the honest truth, Doc. Do
you really think that we can gun down Adams and Tom
Pearson?"

The doctor nodded. "Yes," he said. "If I didn't think that
at least one of our men had a chance of doing it, I wouldn't
bother offering a bounty. You are very fortunate to be alive,
and you still have some of the best guns in Nevada under
your control. Call them into your offices. Let them see how

you have suffered. Fire up their loyalty—if such an emotion even exists among those types—then set the pack free."

"Like a bunch of dogs."

"If you choose to use that analogy, then yes. It wouldn't hurt to send the loggers on a rampage through town. Under some pretense—offer them free whiskey. Let's just see if we make enough things happen we can get lucky and kill the Gunsmith."

"All right," Oatman said. "I'll unleash all the forces I have on them."

The doctor patted his shoulder as he would any recovering patient. "Good. The prognosis for a speedy resolution to this situation is assured. We will recover from today's set-back. Trust your doctor, Jeb."

Jeb Oatman nodded. "I will, sir. I surely will."

TWENTY-EIGHT

Clint and Tom Pearson heard about the one-thousand-dollar bounty almost as soon as it was announced. He and Tom sat grim-faced in the sheriff's office and considered what they might do to protect themselves.

"There really isn't much that can be done," Clint said. "We pledged to the people of this town that we'd bring justice. We can't do that unless we're willing to go out and face whoever has decided that they can earn themselves a bounty."

Tom shook his head. "But how can we protect ourselves from an ambusher's bullet?"

Clint considered the question carefully. "A bounty has been placed on my head by the opposition any number of times and I always managed to survive."

"Keep talking."

Clint laced his fingers behind his head, eased back in the sheriff's swivel chair, and studied the ceiling. "What we have to do," he said, as much to himself as to his new deputy, "is to survive the first attack and leave no doubt in the minds of anyone else that trying to collect a bounty on our hides is a fatal mistake."

"I guess that sounds absolutely reasonable," Tom said, not looking at all convinced.

Clint dropped his heels to the floor. He stood up, and checked his gun, and then walked over to the rifle rack and selected a double-barreled shotgun. "You any kind of a shot?"

"Not much."

"It won't matter with this," Clint said, tossing him the shotgun. He gestured toward the door. "They're already out there somewhere, and they're waiting for us to show up for the dance. So let's not disappoint them. One way or the other, we are going to end this bounty business before the day is over."

"Spoken like a real sheriff," Tom said drily as he followed the Gunsmith out the door and into the street. "We just sort of parade around like a couple of wild turkeys itching to be shot out of our feathers."

"That's the idea," Clint joked. "Only difference is, wild turkeys don't shoot back."

It was ten o'clock at night, and they had been drifting up and down Main Street all afternoon and evening. Clint and Tom knew the gunmen on Oatman's payroll and whenever they came across those men, on the street or in a saloon, there was a tense moment. But so far, nothing had happened.

"I'd like to think they were just afraid of us," Tom said, "but somehow, I don't think that's the case."

"Oh, they're worried all right. But they'll come." Clint stepped inside the Bucket of Blood Saloon and knew that this was the place and the time. There were four gunmen standing against the bar and when he entered, their spines straightened and they stopped talking.

"Why don't we have a beer," Clint said, gestering toward the men so Tom understood.

"Sure. I'm thirsty."

Clint eased up to the bar, and when several of the other patrons who had been drinking suddenly upended their mugs of beer and headed for the door, Clint knew that his instincts had not deceived him.

"Two beers," he called down to the bartender.

The man was at the far end of the bar and he did not seem eager to come down and pour. Clint smiled grimly. "Guess I'll get them myself."

He moved around the bar and found a couple of glasses. The four gunmen were trying hard not to look at him, but their nerves were so stretched that it was almost comic to watch their elaborate pretense.

Clint took his time finding two bottles of beer and then opening them. He saw that Tom had shifted the shotgun into position and was ready. Tom was sweating; his rugged face looked strained but determined. Clint knew that the blacksmith, in a fistfight, could probably whip any three men, but his size and big muscles were a disadvantage in a gunfight. They would combine to slow him down and make him a better target.

Clint did not want Pearson to die. That's why, instead of forcing a violent showdown that was sure to end in bloodshed, the Gunsmith drew his Colt and slammed it down on the bar saying, "Which one of you wants the first case of lead poisoning?"

Three of the gunmen froze, but the man farthest down the bar lost his senses and tried to make his play. Clint aimed to wing the man and did put a bullet through his arm but Tom Pearson just snapped his shotgun up and pulled the trigger.

The explosion was deafening. The gunman was hit by the full force of the blast and lifted completely off his feet, then hurled backward to slam over a table, and finally lay still.

"Easy, Tom!" Clint edged down the bar until he was only a few feet away from the three men. "You have the choice of either going to prison or of signing a confession that Jeb Oatman hired you to kill me and my deputy."

The men stared at the gun in Clint's unwavering fist. They turned and looked at big Tom Pearson and the smoking shotgun in his massive hands. They did not want to look at what a single slug had done to their friend's chest.

"Bartender," Clint hollered. "Get a paper and pen and get down here. You and everyone else in this saloon will be a witness."

Clint got his signed statement, and then he and Tom

escorted the three gunfighters to their horses. "If I ever see any of you in Pine Bluff again, you're as good as dead," he promised.

The three nodded and raced off into the night.

When the sound of their horses' hoofbeats died in the night, Tom said, "What kind of confession is admissible evidence when taken at the point of a gun?"

Clint smiled coldly. "If we go visit Jeb Oatman right now, who is going to tell him how it was obtained?"

"All right," Tom said. "Let's go and finish this up once and for all."

TWENTY-NINE

Word spread fast and, as Clint and Tom marched up the street toward the mansion where Jeb Oatman lay recovering from his wounds, excitement and speculation gathered like a storm about to break. About a dozen loggers had time to grab their axes and guns and came rushing to Oatman's and they were lined up at the mansion's gateway when Clint arrived. A few men held torches up in the air and the tension was almost palpable.

"That's far enough," a burly logger said, stepping forward with his fists knotted and as hard as rocks. "We know who you are and what you want, Gunsmith. Mr. Oatman is our boss and we ain't letting you take him."

"I'm the sheriff and I have a confession that says he put a bounty on my head, and that of Deputy Pearson. I've come to arrest him for that, and for the murder of Abner Turner."

"Elvis Tate killed Turner!"

"And he was hired by Oatman. I have that written down in this confession, too."

The logger shook his head. "You'll have to come through me and if you use your guns, you'll end up swinging from a rope."

Tom Pearson stopped Clint before he could move forward. "I'll handle this," he said in a quiet voice.

Clint did not argue. The logger must have stood six-two and weighed well over two hundred pounds. But when Tom stepped up to the man, the logger seemed to shrink.

Tom doubled up his fists and said, "You want to step aside under your own power or mine?"

The logger cussed and swung his fist. It caught Tom a tremendous blow on the side of the face and he staggered. The logger took heart and swung again, but this time, Tom ducked and ripped an uppercut to the logger's belly that made his cheeks puff out. Tom grabbed him by the throat and threw him right over the picket fence into a bed of roses. The logger bellowed in pain and when he came to his feet, it was to take off running.

"Who is next?" Tom asked in a quiet, dangerous voice.

Not a single logger or gunfighter wanted any part of Tom or Clint. In the first case, there was not a man among them who could match Tom's fists, in the second case, Clint's gun reigned supreme.

"Let's arrest the man we came for," Clint said, pushing past the men and heading for the door. He did not knock when he stepped up to the house but just grabbed the doorknob and twisted.

"It's locked."

Tom gently brushed him aside. He reared back and kicked the door in and they came through. Clint said, "You check downstairs, I'll go up."

Clint grabbed the staircase railing and yelled, "It's all over, Oatman. I've got a signed confession that says you were the one that ordered Abner Turner shot to death. Also that you put a bounty on us. Come on down with your hands in the air!"

There was no answer so Clint started to climb. He was halfway up the stairs with a gun in one hand and the signed confession in the other before Oatman suddenly jumped into view at the top of the stairs and opened fire with a pearl-handled revolver.

His bullet nicked Clint in the ear. Clint twisted and fired in one motion, and his bullet caught Oatman in the solar plexus and lifted him up on the toes of his feet. Oatman's face went blank, but he was still trying to raise his gun when his legs buckled. He pitched forward and came tumbling down the stairs. His body hit the Gunsmith and took his legs out from under him, and together they rolled down to the hallway.

Tom grabbed Clint and pulled him to his feet. "Are you all right?"

Clint hugged his ribs. "I think my ribs were well on the road to mend, but that sure didn't help them any."

"Dr. Potter is out of town, but old Doc Cutter lives just a few miles up the mountain from here. He's Oatman's friend but maybe I should still send for him."

"It wouldn't hurt," Clint said, feeling waves of pain. "Ask someone to go for the man."

Tom disappeared for a few minutes only to return and help Clint into Oatman's library and a leather-covered easy chair. Clint spied a decanter of brandy and said, "Why don't you pour us a couple of shots? It's probably expensive stuff, given Oatman's standard of living."

"I don't drink," Tom said, "but I'll be happy to pour you a glass."

"So this is the end," he said a few minutes later. "We've won."

Clint shrugged. "Looks like, but I'd feel a whole lot better if you'd go outside and explain to the loggers why it had to work out this way."

"They'll never believe me."

"Yes, they will," Clint said, sipping on the excellent brandy. "Read them the confession and tell them that Pine Bluff wants their business for a whole lot longer than they'd have been here if the mountainside was stripped clean. They'll understand."

But Tom was not too confident. "I'm not real good with words, Gunsmith. I'm a lot better with my hands than I am with my tongue."

"That will change." Clint smiled. "I expect that when you and Milly are married, you'll do a lot more listening than talking anyway."

"She told you we were getting married!"

Clint managed a thin smile. "Yeah."

"My God, you've just made me the happiest man in the world!"

Clint extended his glass in a token salute. He had no concern whatsoever that some gunman would try and shoot the deputy. With Oatman dead, the bounty was no longer in effect. "Why don't you get out there and settle the crowd. We can celebrate some other time."

Tom Pearson hurried outside. Clint heard him begin to talk to the loggers whose respect he had won only a few minutes earlier. He told them about the way people felt concerning Pine Bluff and their town. And how it wasn't right to strip the mountainsides.

Clint listened for a few minutes and then he pushed himself to his feet and walked over to pour himself another glass of brandy. His ribs hurt like hell and he was hoping that the doctor had something to give him for the pain.

It seemed like hours before Cutter arrived. The man was ushered inside and when he saw Jeb Oatman lying dead at the foot of the stairs, he paled and knelt by his side. He opened the dead man's coat and then unbuttoned his shirt and studied the bullet hole. Something terrible in his expression warned Clint that this man had been very close to Oatman.

Doc Cutter struggled and managed to regain his composure. "So," he said, "you *have* won."

Clint's eyes narrowed. "Not me, the people of Pine Bluff."

The doctor came over to him. "The man said something about your ribs. Please remove your coat and shirt."

Clint did as he was ordered. The doctor examined him for a moment and said, "They're cracked, not broken. But you must be in a great deal of pain."

"I have felt better."

Doc Cutter smiled. "Of course. I have something here for

you. It's a painkiller in the form of an elixir. It should fix you right up."

Clint watched the man take a bottle from his medicine bag and uncork it. When he handed it to the Gunsmith, Clint could feel a wetness indicating that the painkiller had just been concocted.

"You can drink it straight from the bottle, or, if you prefer, I'll go to the kitchen for a spoon."

"I'll finish my brandy first," Clint said. "Then I'll take a dose a little later."

Cutter started to reach for Clint's glass of brandy. "I'm afraid narcotics and brandy do not mix well," he said.

Clint did not give the man his drink, and when Cutter tried to forceably pull it from his hand, Clint pretended to accidently knock the bottle of elixir over to the floor, where it shattered.

"You fool!" the doctor shouted. "Look what you've done!"

"Sorry," Clint said in a tight voice. "I don't think I'll need your services after all, Doctor."

The man was shaking with fury as he snapped his bag shut and marched out the door. He stopped once more to study the body of Jeb Oatman, then he left.

I wouldn't drink something he concocted for love nor money, Clint thought, staring at the broken glass and the dark puddle on the floor.

THIRTY

Two weeks had passed, and Pine Bluff was having a big Fourth of July celebration. It was remarkable how, once Oatman and his gunfighters had been taken care of, the town no longer seemed to be divided between two camps—the loggers against the ranchers, farmers, and small businesses.

Tom Pearson and Milly Turner had announced their engagement and the blacksmith had reshod Duke. The sky was clear and powder blue over the towering Sierra Nevada Mountains and down below, the fiddle music was loud and lively. But Clint figured it was time to go on to San Francisco.

He saddled Duke and tied the big gelding up at the town hall where the town council was meeting to elect a new sheriff. Tom Pearson had considered the job, but Clint had convinced the big man to decline. Tom was better suited to his own trade and his hands were going to be busy helping Milly run her ranch. Juan Escobar had left for Mexico, and Milly had decided to sell all but a few lambs and try her hand at cattle ranching.

Things changed, Clint thought, as he stood beside Dora's grave in the little cemetery on the hillside. Directly below him was the town hall and Clint could hear but not distinguish the words of Archibald MacDonald as he spoke in behalf of his choice for sheriff. Pine Bluff was a fine town, a town that would endure and attract good men.

The Gunsmith knelt beside Dora's fresh grave and studied it. He was reluctant to leave her for she had saved his life despite the fact that the last time he had seen her alive he had chided her for not understanding his ideals.

"I had no right to do that, Dora," the Gunsmith said quietly. "You loved me and I loved you. I wished I could have taken you over to the Barbary Coast with me. We always talked about going there together, and you would have liked the restaurants and the little seafood vendors along the wharf. I'm sorry and I'll never forget you, or Pine Bluff."

Clint lapsed into silence for a few minutes. He breathed deeply of the pines and he could see far out over the broad Carson Valley. Western Nevada was good country, beautiful country, and if he had been a marrying sort, he would have married Milly Turner and had himself a nice ranch, maybe a family before too many years. But he was a loner, a drifter, a gambler who preferred adventure and a fresh piece of scenery as often as possible.

Clint started to mount Duke and ride away. He had said his good-byes to the people in town that mattered to him. And he'd more than likely be coming back through in a while to visit again. But he'd never find another woman who had loved him like Dora.

As Clint shoved his foot into the stirrup, something out of the ordinary caught his attention. He put his foot back down to earth and studied the tall, thin man who had quietly sneaked around behind the meeting hall where he could not be seen. Though the day was very warm, the man wore an overcoat and now, he reached into his pocket and very slowly pulled out a bottle. With great care, and holding the bottle with both hands, the secretive man knelt and placed the bottle just under the hall's flooring where only part of it could be seen.

It was Doc Cutter!

A warning sounded in Clint's mind. He led Duke into the

cover of trees so that they could not be seen. Cutter finished inspecting his secretive work and then he looked up toward Clint and the little Pine Bluff Cemetery. Seeing no one, he appeared to be satisfied. He removed his coat and draped it over his arm, then strolled around to join the celebration.

Clint scratched his head with curiosity. Something was definitely afoot and it wasn't good. Tying Duke in the trees, Clint walked downhill to the meeting hall. With his injured ribs, he bent at the knees and reached under the building a few inches and retrieved the bottle. Staring at it, he felt his hands begin to shake a little. He had seen nitroglycerine before but he'd never wanted to see it again. It was a thick, yellow mixture that had a unique coloring that was not easily forgotten. Clint pressed the bottle to his body and cradled it like an egg.

"That crazy doctor plans to shoot it and blow up the town hall meeting!" he whispered to himself.

The enormity of the murder intended by Doc Cutter was enough to make Clint seethe with fury. No doubt the doctor was planning on circulating for a few minutes with all the other celebrants before taking a vantage point up near the cemetery and then shooting the bottle and blowing half the population of Pine Bluff all to hell.

The Gunsmith knew that he had to act quickly. He took the bottle and gently poured half of its contents into the dirt where it soaked in and disappeared. Then, he hid the bottle and went around front of the meeting hall to join the celebration. It took only a minute to find an empty whiskey bottle and he hurried back around and placed it where the bottle of nitroglycerine had been.

Now came the dicey part. Clint retrieved what remained of the real nitroglycerine and hurried back up the hill toward his horse. He understood that if he slipped and fell, he would blow himself into a million pieces. But he didn't fall and when he reached Duke, he hid in the trees and waited.

Sure enough, Doc Cutter appeared less than fifteen minutes later. He moved across the mountainside until he was almost directly below Clint and hidden in the trees. The Gunsmith watched grimly as the doctor settled in about thirty yards below the cemetery and took aim with a rifle.

Doc Cutter aimed very, very carefully down the mountainside and when he unleashed a bullet, Clint saw the glass bottle he had planted burst.

But there was no explosion.

Doc Cutter could not believe it! He actually stood up in plain sight and fired again, though at what, the Gunsmith could not imagine. Swearing, Cutter dropped his rifle and ducked into the trees on the run.

Clint had seen enough. With the nitroglycerine tucked into his saddlebag, he mounted Duke and rode the gelding deeper into the forest. He dared not hurry after Cutter, but then, he didn't figure that would be necessary. Cutter was old, soft and slow.

Clint overtook the man within a mile. Cutter was still about forty yards below him and he was breathing hard. "Hey!" Clint yelled, reaching for the bottle of nitroglycerine. "You forgot this. Catch!"

The doctor was in a high state of agitation and his exertion no doubt contributed to his momentary confusion at the sight of the Gunsmith mounted on his horse up above. And as Clint gently lobbed the half-filled bottle of nitroglycerine toward him, Doc Cutter did make a valiant attempt to catch it. But the trail was narrow and the footing slick with pine needles.

Clint did not wait to see the doctor lunging with outstretched arms toward the downward arcing bottle of yellow fluid. He drove his spurs into Duke and the big horse shot up the mountainside like a seared goat. Even so, when the huge explosion rocked the forest, Clint felt its blast and, for an instant, it was like being struck by a tornado as limbs, pinecones, rocks, and brush were pulverized and sprayed outward from a crater where Doc Cutter missed his last catch.

Clint let Duke run though the dark forest. In a short while,

ere would be a crowd standing around that big hole in the
ountainside. The Gunsmith wondered if there would even
a piece of Doc Cutter to give the spectators even more
use to wonder, or if they would just figure that some
unken celebrant had a fatal accident with a monster fire-
acker.

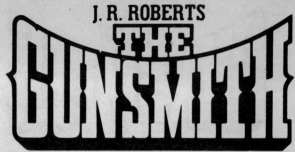

J. R. ROBERTS
THE GUNSMITH
SERIES

☐ 0-441-30932-1	THE GUNSMITH #1: MACKLIN'S WOMEN	$2.50
☐ 0-441-30930-5	THE GUNSMITH #7: THE LONGHORN WAR	$2.50
☐ 0-441-30931-3	THE GUNSMITH #11: ONE-HANDED GUN	$2.50
☐ 0-441-30905-4	THE GUNSMITH #15: BANDIT GOLD	$2.50
☐ 0-441-30907-0	THE GUNSMITH #17: SILVER WAR	$2.50
☐ 0-441-30913-5	THE GUNSMITH #30: THE PONDEROSA WAR	$2.50
☐ 0-441-30949-6	THE GUNSMITH #45: NAVAHO DEVIL	$2.50
☐ 0-441-30952-6	THE GUNSMITH #48: ARCHER'S REVENGE	$2.50
☐ 0-441-30953-4	THE GUNSMITH #49: SHOWDOWN IN RATON	$2.50
☐ 0-441-30955-0	THE GUNSMITH #51: DESERT HELL	$2.50
☐ 0-441-30956-9	THE GUNSMITH #52: THE DIAMOND GUN	$2.50
☐ 0-441-30957-7	THE GUNSMITH #53: DENVER DUO	$2.50
☐ 0-441-30958-5	THE GUNSMITH #54: HELL ON WHEELS	$2.50
☐ 0-441-30959-3	THE GUNSMITH #55: THE LEGEND MAKER	$2.50

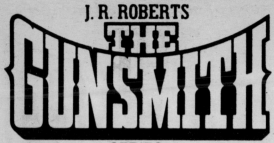

J. R. ROBERTS
THE GUNSMITH

SERIES

☐ 0-441-30962-3	THE GUNSMITH #58: THE DEADLY HEALER	$2.50
☐ 0-441-30964-X	THE GUNSMITH #60: GERONIMO'S TRAIL	$2.50
☐ 0-441-30965-8	THE GUNSMITH #61: THE COMSTOCK GOLD FRAUD	$2.50
☐ 0-441-30966-6	THE GUNSMITH #62: BOOM TOWN KILLER	$2.50
☐ 0-441-30967-4	THE GUNSMITH #63: TEXAS TRACKDOWN	$2.50
☐ 0-441-30968-2	THE GUNSMITH #64: THE FAST DRAW LEAGUE	$2.50
☐ 0-441-30969-0	THE GUNSMITH #65: SHOWDOWN IN RIO MALO	$2.50
☐ 0-441-30970-4	THE GUNSMITH #66: OUTLAW TRAIL	$2.50
☐ 0-515-09058-1	THE GUNSMITH #67: HOMESTEADER GUNS	$2.75
☐ 0-515-09118-9	THE GUNSMITH #68: FIVE CARD DEATH	$2.75
☐ 0-515-09176-6	THE GUNSMITH #69: TRAIL DRIVE TO MONTANA	$2.75
☐ 0-515-09258-4	THE GUNSMITH #70: TRIAL BY FIRE	$2.75
☐ 0-515-09217-7	THE GUNSMITH #71: THE OLD WHISTLER GANG	$2.75
☐ 0-515-09329-7	THE GUNSMITH #72: DAUGHTER OF GOLD	$2.75
☐ 0-515-09380-7	THE GUNSMITH #73: APACHE GOLD	$2.75
☐ 0-515-09447-1	THE GUNSMITH #74: PLAINS MURDER	$2.75
☐ 0-515-09493-5	THE GUNSMITH #75: DEADLY MEMORIES	$2.75
☐ 0-515-09523-0	THE GUNSMITH #76: THE NEVADA TIMBER WAR	$2.75
☐ 0-515-09550-8	THE GUNSMITH #77: NEW MEXICO SHOW DOWN	$2.75
☐ 0-515-09587-7	THE GUNSMITH #78: BARBED WIRE AND BULLETS (On sale June '88)	$2.95
☐ 0-515-09649-0	THE GUNSMITH #79: DEATH EXPRESS (On sale July '88)	$2.95

Please send the titles I've checked above. Mail orders to:

BERKLEY PUBLISHING GROUP
390 Murray Hill Pkwy., Dept. B
East Rutherford, NJ 07073

NAME _____

ADDRESS _____

CITY _____

STATE _____ ZIP _____

Please allow 6 weeks for delivery.
Prices are subject to change without notice.

POSTAGE & HANDLING:
$1.00 for one book, $.25 for each
additional. Do not exceed $3.50.

BOOK TOTAL $ _____

SHIPPING & HANDLING $ _____

APPLICABLE SALES TAX $ _____
(CA, NJ, NY, PA)

TOTAL AMOUNT DUE $ _____
PAYABLE IN US FUNDS.
(No cash orders accepted.)